# Running
# Scared

M AC  B OWERS

iUniverse, Inc.
Bloomington

# Running Scared

*Copyright © 2011 by Mac Bowers*

*This is a work of fiction. All of the characters, names, incidents, organizations, and dialogue in this novel are either the products of the author's imagination or are used fictitiously.*

*iUniverse books may be ordered through booksellers or by contacting:*

*iUniverse*
*1663 Liberty Drive*
*Bloomington, IN 47403*
*www.iuniverse.com*
*1-800-Authors (1-800-288-4677)*

*ISBN: 978-1-4620-8380-0 (sc)*
*ISBN: 978-1-4620-8382-4 (hc)*
*ISBN: 978-1-4620-8381-7 (e)*

*Printed in the United States of America*

*iUniverse rev. date: 1/9/2012*

# Prologue

A year ago, I couldn't drive. I still lived in a large California city, and I was trying my best to be known, to stand out. Now, everything's changed. I drive myself to and from school. I live in the middle of nowhere—otherwise known as Mistle, Pennsylvania. And now I'm trying to blend in.

In one year, everything changed. I had no idea so much could take place in such a short time. Why did this have to happen to me?

# Chapter 1

That morning, on my first day in Mistle, Mom insisted on driving me to school. I tried firmly reminding her that I could now drive myself, but she wouldn't hear of it.

You'd think that the middle of August in Pennsylvania would be bright and warm. But no, that day seemed to coincidently fit my mood. Rain pelted the windshield, and the wiper blades raced to clear Mom's view. Staring out the window, I watched the pavement, glossy with water, speed under us. We were late. As usual.

"Morgan?" Mom's velvety voice sounded like she didn't notice the weather. Or my mood. I looked at her expectantly. She knew I was listening. "Try to be happy today, okay? I know you didn't want to move. But you'll make friends." We pulled up to the front of the school, and she turned in her seat to face me. "I know last year was ... rough, for you, sweetie. But things are okay now." She reached for my hand, but I jerked away.

It wasn't that I didn't want her comfort. Because I did. I needed it, craved it even. But, looking down at my hands, I saw the evidence of what happened last year before we moved from California. My lifelines, the lines that marked the palms of my hands, were pale and puffy with scar tissue. I balled my hands into fists and squeezed my eyes shut. I hated remembering. I never wanted to remember again.

Then I opened my eyes and shot Mom the fakest smile she'll ever see. "I know, Mom. It's all over now. It's all good. I'm happy."

She smiled genuinely. If she noticed my fake one, she didn't want to acknowledge it. She reached her hand out, like she wanted to touch me, but hesitantly pulled it back at the last second. "Have a good day."

I nodded and got out of the cramped car. As she drove away, I ascended the steps to my new high school.

Right after I stepped in the door, I heard, "Will Morgan Casey please report to the office?" I briefly wondered if they had been waiting for me, but made my way to the room that looked like it would be the office anyway. Once inside, I was greeted by the secretary. She gave me a cheesy smile, and in a bubbly voice, said, "Welcome to Mistle High School. My name is Mrs. Mason." Even though she told me, I sneaked a peek at the nameplate on her desk. Sure enough, it read, "Mrs. Mason." The incident from last year had taught me to trust no one. Mrs. Mason handed me a stack of papers with a nametag on top that read, "Morgan Casey."

"Umm," I said hesitantly, not sure how to begin my lie. "My last name is spelled wrong." I pushed the nametag toward her. "It's supposed to be spelled K-a-s-i-e." I held my breath. She was the first person I was trying this out on, and if it didn't work, I was in deep trouble.

Mrs. Mason frowned. "That's funny. The paperwork your other school faxed us doesn't spell it that way."

"Well, they must have made a mistake," I insisted.

Mrs. Mason plastered a smile on her face that said, "This kid is going to be a pain." But aloud, she said, "Okay, we'll fix that for you. In the meantime, you can take a tour of the school. Charlie should be here in a minute. Oh, here he is now."

As if on cue, a tall, blond-haired boy sauntered into the office. He wore a contagious smile, accompanied by smile lines. A sure sign he smiled a lot. He walked up to me, hand extended, still smiling.

"Hi, I'm Charlie. You're the new girl, right?" He stood waiting for me to shake his hand, but I didn't. I balled the ends of my hoodie sleeves in my hands and nodded.

"Morgan," I mumbled.

"Oh." Charlie's smile faltered a bit but never left his face. "Nice to meet you. I'm supposed to give you a tour, hang out with you a bit until you make some friends. Know what I mean?"

"Sure."

Charlie led me out of the office, and we walked down the hallway together. "Or, even if you do make friends, I could stick around if you want me to."

"Whatever."

The whole way around the school, Charlie never stopped talking. I wondered how the kid got enough oxygen to stay alive. We were almost at the other end of the school before Charlie realized I was only giving him one-word answers, and that was only if I had to say anything at all. Which I didn't, for the most part.

"You don't talk much, do you?" Charlie stopped walking to study me closely.

I stopped beside him, letting my hair fall over my eyes, stuffing my hands into my pockets, uneasy under his scrutiny. "No."

Charlie beamed and started walking again. I followed. "Well," he said, "we're just going to have to change that."

I wasn't sure what he meant by that. But he didn't give any explanation, and I didn't ask for any. We toured the school, and I mostly tuned Charlie out. All I could hear was the buzzing of his incessant voice, our footsteps thudding on the tiled floor, and my own thoughts. No matter what Charlie said, I was planning on keeping to myself. I couldn't afford to have friends. I didn't want any.

# Chapter 2

As I roamed the halls on my first day of school, absently going from class to class (with Charlie as my guide), I tried to trick myself into thinking I was just a normal girl, living a normal life, not hiding a not so normal secret. When I walked into a new classroom with a new teacher, full of new faces, I tried to ignore the blatant staring and the not so hushed whispers all around me. But even as I refused to think about my unfamiliar surroundings or to look at my hands, I wasn't fooling myself. All of this was new. I wasn't the girl I was last year. And I couldn't seem to forget that fact.

My classes flew by effortlessly. No one expects the new kid to answer questions, and homework was done during the next class as the hours ticked by. All in all, my first day at Mistle High School didn't end in catastrophe.

After school, I stood outside for an hour, waiting for Mom to come pick me up. An hour turned into an hour and a half. Then two hours. I contemplated walking home, but looking up at the gray sky, I saw that it would be dark soon, and it looked like it wanted to rain again.

*Who cares?* I swore under my breath and started for the road. About a mile into the walk, a blue sedan pulled up beside me. My breath came in short gasps, and memories flashed in front of my eyes.

The sound of the engine. "She's the one. She knows." Voices. Then a cold hand gripping my arm, not letting go even as I screamed and struggled. Threats—I remembered I made threats. The whole time, I never stopped screaming. No one helped me. Then a blindfold tied over my eyes, a cloth covering my nose and mouth, commands to breathe, a sickly sweet smell. Then. Nothing. But. Blackness.

Back to the present, I quickened my pace, not daring to glance over my shoulder back at the car. Now, I was running. Sprinting like crazy. Never stopping. Forgetting to breathe. My shoelace caught a crack in the sidewalk. I went sprawling. In a tangle of arms and legs, I fell to the ground. *It's over*, I thought while lying there. *I'm done for.* A shadow loomed over me, and I closed my eyes, preparing myself for the worst.

"Morgan?"

My eyes flew open at the familiar voice. "Charlie," I croaked. A sigh of relief left my lips in a whoosh. Charlie extended his hand to help me up. I ignored it, sat up, and then climbed to my feet myself.

"Are you okay?" Charlie asked. His brow was furrowed in a way that showed he was genuinely concerned. It was sweet.

"I'm fine. Really," I assured him.

The worry lines in his forehead disappeared. "You took a nasty fall," he said. Then he grabbed my wrists and turned my hands over to inspect them. What I saw made me nauseous. Blood smeared my palms. It oozed out of the scrapes and dripped delicately to the ground. My head began to spin. I heard the voices again.

"Make her tell!" That particular voice sounded so frustrated. "I don't care what it takes! Make. Her. Tell!" A door slammed. Something clinked. My hands were turned over. I felt a searing pain.

"Whoa." Charlie dropped my hands and gripped my shoulders. "You don't look so hot. Let me take you home." I fervently shook my head and ripped his hands off me. Then I fell to my knees and retched on the sidewalk.

Charlie wordlessly held back my hair as I threw up my stomach contents. When I was done, I sat back on my heels and took deep, shaky breaths.

"Could ... could you get me a napkin?" I asked.

Charlie nodded and opened his car door. I heard him rummaging through something before he reappeared with a handful of Wendy's napkins.

"Here." He handed them to me. I mumbled thanks before wiping my palms with them, careful to get every drop of blood. Charlie watched, looking puzzled. I knew what he was thinking without having to ask him. A normal person would have wiped her mouth with the napkins. But I'll never be normal again.

"Come on." Charlie gently took my elbow and helped me stand up. "Let's get you home."

# Chapter 3

So, Charlie drove me home. The only conversation in the car was when he asked for directions to my house, which I gave him before quieting again. And Charlie didn't seem to be able to think of anything to say. He must have talked himself out during our tour.

Actually, the ride was almost awkward. Charlie kept glancing at me out of the corner of his eye, as if checking to see if I was still all right. I was. Or maybe he was just seeing whether or not he was going to have to stop to let me out if I decided I needed to throw up all over his car. Either way, I didn't like the attention.

"Is this it?" Charlie pulled up next to my simple, two-story house with the peeled white paint and porch that badly needed fixing.

"Yup." My lips made a popping sound on the *p*. I reached for the door handle.

"Want me to walk you in?"

I opened the car door a crack and listened. Sure enough, a loud crash that sounded like breaking glass echoed from my house, and I just barely heard raised voices. Maybe it was safer for him to just go home.

"No." I hoped I wasn't being rude. I thought about adding "thanks" at the end, but that sounded too friendly. And I did not want to be Charlie's friend.

"Okay. See you at school tomorrow?"

I nodded and climbed out of the car. Charlie drove away slowly, hesitantly it seemed like, and as soon as he was gone, I made my way to the front door. As soon as I swung it open, the voices hushed and the whole house became eerily silent. I sighed and rolled my eyes. Walking into the kitchen, I saw Mom and Dad standing in the middle of the room. Mom's face was red, and her eyes were glassy. Dad clenched and unclenched his fists and threw me a forced smile.

"Hi, Morgan!" I wished he could hear just how fake he sounded. He opened his arms to hug me, but I just stood there. Slowly, he lowered them. "How was school, sweetheart?"

"Fine."

Neither of them even asked how I got home. Mom probably didn't even know that she forgot me. She was probably too focused on screaming at Dad. I wondered what they had broken and how they had hid it so quickly.

So there the three of us stood. Mom shooting daggers at Dad when she thought I wasn't looking, Dad looking at me like everything in our lives was perfect, and me staring at them, wondering how they could pretend so easily. After several long minutes of that, I announced, "I'm going to bed."

"Without dinner?" Mom asked.

I nodded. "I ate a big lunch." So maybe I lied, but they believed me. I was getting good at it. Without waiting for them to say anything, I headed upstairs.

My bedroom was small. That's all there is to it. It was big enough to fit my single bed, my nightstand, and my dresser. That left barely enough space to move around. But at least it had a door with a lock on it. And the two windows locked. I felt safer in this room.

Quickly, I changed into my pajamas and climbed into bed. And just—lay there. There wasn't much else to do. I didn't like sleep. With it, it brought memories and dreams and time to think. All of which I neither wanted nor needed. So I stared up at the ceiling and listened to my parents argue.

"No, Michele, this whole thing is not my fault!"

It's been the same thing for the past year.

"You let our daughter grow apart from us, Ben! How is it not your fault?" Mom sounded hysterical. "She's upstairs in her bed probably having nightmares about last year! You were the one with her when that whole incident occurred!"

Dad screamed, "What was I supposed to do? She isn't five anymore! I should be able to turn my back for ten minutes and trust that she can take care of herself!"

Maybe that was the problem. Maybe I couldn't take care of myself.

Now Mom's voice was icy cold, signaling an end to tonight's fight. "Because of you, our little girl's life has been turned upside down. And she will never be able to forget it. She has to live with the proof every day."

"Just go to bed, Michele." I could picture Dad shaking his head, a movement to go along with his tired voice. "Just go to bed."

They were done. For tonight at least. I already knew tomorrow night wouldn't be any different. This has been our routine for the past year now.

In the darkness, I looked down at my hands. The blood from my spill on the sidewalk earlier was gone. But the scar tissue stood out plainly in the blackness. Mom was right; I was never going to forget the event that changed my life last year. There was no way I could. Not when the reminder was right in front of me.

I balled my hands up and stuffed them under my pillow. I wasn't going to be reminded the rest of the night. If I had it my way, I wouldn't be reminded for the rest of my life. But getting my way just wasn't something that happened to me anymore.

# Chapter 4

All I saw was darkness, nothing but pitch black. All around me. Blinding me. Suffocating me. Enveloping me. But strangely, I didn't feel fear. Inch by inch, I blindly staggered forward. My mind had no idea where I was going, but my legs had a determined destination.

A sudden bright light caused me to recoil back, but I put my arm up to shield my eyes and pressed on.

Then I was in a dimly lit room. A basement. With a cold, unforgiving cement floor and cement blocks for walls. No windows and only one door placed at the top of a long staircase that stretched on forever. And suddenly, I felt fear.

It gripped at my stomach and shook my hands, scrambling my brain and disrupting any logical thoughts. I heard a scream, and it might have been me, but I wasn't sure.

Suddenly, I wasn't alone in the basement anymore. In the middle of the room lay a girl, my age, with brown eyes and short red hair that fell just below her ears. I felt a smile tugging on the corners of my mouth. A thousand words popped into my head at once to describe the scene. Amazing. Miracle. Captivating. All happy memories of playing in the rain, camping trips, slumber parties, hot summers, birthdays.

"Jamie!" I called. The girl sat up and smiled shyly at me. Then got to her feet and ran toward me, as if remembering who I was. And we hugged for the longest time.

"Morgan!" Jamie laughed giddily. And I laughed with her.

Then, I remembered fights, secrets, separation. And my smile faltered. The laughter stopped.

"They're coming," Jamie whispered in my ear, and more memories flashed in front of my eyes. Promises kept, others broken, violence and police, a hospital and a church. I gasped and stumbled out of my best friend's arms. She smiled at me, only this time it was an evil, bone-chilling smile. I shuddered. Then she opened her mouth, tilted her head up, and let out a shrill scream that didn't sound human. And then she vanished. Desperately, I darted for the door, only to find that with each stair I took, a new one appeared, preventing me from reaching the safety at the top. Forever keeping me in the darkness of the basement.

Mercifully, I was back in my bed. Sweat plastered my hair to my face. I felt frozen. My sheets were in a giant heap on the floor. I grabbed one and pulled it over me. Slowly, I warmed up. But my whole body shook violently, and not from the cold. I took a deep breath and tried to clear the images of the surreal dream from my head. My lifelines ached. Pulling one of my pillows to my chest, I bit down on it, screaming for the rest of the night. And prayed for sunlight.

# Chapter 5

It wasn't going to be a good day. I knew that even before I walked out the door. Memories of my dream from the night before still haunted me. And I missed my best friend.

I couldn't remember when I had met Jamie; it was when I was just a baby. Our mom's met at a park that we often went to. I guess they clicked and spent a lot of time together, meaning Jamie and I spent a lot of time together. Funny how things turn out.

My earliest memory of Jamie had to be just before we started kindergarten. Maybe even earlier. We were playing at the same park our mom's met at. Our favorite game back then was house, just like every other little girl's was. Jamie and I pretended that we were twin sisters, living in an enormous mansion with nothing to do but play and have fun. In our play world, it was lunch time and we agreed she would make me something, and I would make her something. We used the only thing available, mud and worms, to make our lunches. And we both ate it. All of it. Worms and everything. That night, I spent the night at Jamie's house. We both ended up getting sick. Really sick. Her mother called my mother, and they were both up with us until five in the morning, holding our long hair back as we emptied our stomachs of the foul "lunch." We were afraid of mud from then on, up until the end of second grade.

Walking to my car, I smiled at the memory. When Jamie wasn't around, my world was black and white. I didn't see shades of gray. There was no in between. But when it was the two of us, I was lost in a sea of color.

My world was black and white.

I was starting to get the new school routine down. First period: droning teacher, homework. Second period: droning teacher, more homework. Third period: a droning teacher that thought he was funny, get homework done from first and second period. Study hall: the buzzing of other people's conversations. Lunch: sitting with Charlie and only half paying attention to what he was saying. Sixth period: the kind of teacher that looked like he didn't want to be there anymore than we did, no homework. Seventh period: yet another droning teacher, enough homework to take up my evening. Eighth period: a too peppy teacher and no homework. Ninth period: gym.

I didn't have anything against PE; I just didn't like it very much. It made me feel like everyone was constantly watching me. And I hated that. And we ran all the time. The teacher ran us until we were sick to our stomachs and doubled over, trying to fill our fire-filled lungs with air. Even the really fit kids, who probably ran over a mile before school every morning, had sweat plastered to their faces and flushed cheeks and were breathing hard.

With about five minutes left of school, our drill sergeant decided she was having a good day and let us talk until we were dismissed.

"Morgan!" Charlie shuffled over to me, looking too tired to even pick up his feet.

I looked at the floor. "Hi, Charlie."

"Well, we haven't scared you off yet."

I whipped my head up, but Charlie was grinning, showing he was only teasing. I lowered my eyes again.

"Think you'll stay awhile?"

Could I stay awhile? Did I dare risk it? Or would I have to uproot myself and move across the country again? I didn't know how to answer his question, so I just shrugged my shoulders.

That obviously wasn't the answer he was expecting. I could see that just by the way he looked at me. But what did he want me to say? "Yes, I'm planning on staying here forever and ever!" Yeah … right.

"So, do you have a lot of homework?" Charlie never seemed to run out of things to say.

I rolled my eyes. "Just enough to last forever. Mr. Cannon has no life, or else he wouldn't give us that much homework because he's the one that has to grade it!"

Charlie busted out with laughter. "Nice choice of words," he said through chuckles. For the first time that day, I smiled a little. When he was done laughing, Charlie said, "You know, I'm good at science. I could help you if you want me to."

The truth was, I didn't want him to. Something in the back of my head told me it was a bad idea. Or maybe it was just a habit to deny any help.

"I could use all the help I can get."

# Chapter 6

I was a mess of chemical compounds and genetic punnett squares. Charlie and I were settled in the living room. I was sitting on the couch, a science book open in my lap. Charlie was on the floor at my feet. He was scribbling something scientific that I didn't understand into an open notebook. There was a warm kind of silence that echoed throughout the room. It was the comfortable kind. The kind that didn't need to be broken.

Occasionally, I could hear Charlie's pencil as it scratched along the paper while I turned the pages in the book, reading the material but not understanding a word of it. Eventually I stopped even trying, letting go of all hope that I was ever going to pass tenth-grade science.

"You stuck?" Charlie asked, looking up from his notebook.

"No. I just give up," I said, tossing my textbook on the end of the couch. It bounced once and landed on the floor with a muffled thump.

"You can't exactly 'give up' a required class," Charlie said with a chuckle. He reached over and picked up the book, brushed pretend-dust off it with his hand, and then handed it back to me. When I didn't take it immediately, he pushed it my way once more and said, "I'll help you."

Sighing, I reluctantly took it back and slid myself onto the floor beside him. He flipped it open to the pages we had to read and answer questions on for homework.

"Balancing chemical equations," he said, "is easier than it seems." He ripped a piece of paper out of his notebook and wrote:

$$Ag + H_2S \; Ag_2S + H_2$$
$$2\,(Ag) + H_2S \; Ag_2S + H_2$$

I still didn't get it, and I told him so. "Look," he said, using his pencil as a pointer, "for this problem, just add everything to Ag except for the element, in this case H." I nodded, although the whole lesson just went right over my head. Charlie raised his eyebrows at me. "You still aren't understanding any of this, are you?"

"No," I said bluntly.

Charlie laughed and closed the book so quickly it made a slapping noise when it shut. "Then I guess you're Mr. Cannon's problem." I almost winced but looked at Charlie's face first. The wide grin that lit up his green eyes gave it all away. He was just kidding. "So, what do you say we be done with science?"

"You mean give up a required class?" I teased, pretending to be astonished. Charlie's grin grew. "For today," he allowed.

"For today," I repeated.

"So, what was up with you today?" Charlie suddenly asked. "I mean, I get the whole new school, new people, homesick type deal. But you looked, I don't know. You just looked really sad. Like you'd lost your best friend or something."

I drew in a sharp breath and glared at Charlie, which I knew was unfair. There was no way he could have known. And something told me that if I told him the truth right then, he would regret saying what he did and apologize profoundly. With that in mind, I softened my gaze and opened my mouth to say some smart-aleck reply, but the front door opening interrupted me. Instinctively, I thought about running and slamming the door closed on whoever was letting themselves into the house. But I fought my first reaction and forced myself to take a deep breath.

"Welcome home?" I called curiously.

"Welcome home," my mom's voice confirmed from the doorway. Charlie looked at me funny, but I didn't offer an explanation. It was none of his business anyway. With Charlie trailing behind me, I went to greet Mom.

"How much would you bet me that your father forgot it was his turn to pick up dinner tonight? Double that if he forgets where the only pizza place in town is." Mom had her head bent, focused on getting her shoes off. "What do you want me to make, Morgan? We have ..." She looked up, and her voice trailed off when she saw Charlie. "Hi," she said, giving me the look that said, "Who is this boy, and why is he in our house?"

I hurried to make introductions. "Charlie, this is Mom. Mom, this is Charlie ..." My own voice trailed off. It occurred to me that I didn't even know his last name. I mentally cursed myself for being so careless. Charlie could have been anyone. I couldn't afford to make a mistake like that.

"Ames," Charlie supplied with a charming smile, which I was noticing he saved only for when he met new people. He started to extend his hand but seemed to remember our first encounter, how I wouldn't shake his hand, and pulled it back again. That is, until Mom extended hers. He grinned after shaking her hand. "Phew! I was starting to think you guys didn't do that." Again, he was just kidding. His face said it all. But he had a bad habit of saying the wrong things even when he didn't know any better.

Mom shot me a look. Without me telling her, she knew what had happened. She smiled politely at Charlie. "So you're a friend from school?"

"I don't know. Ask Morgan." Charlie was still smiling as he nodded in my direction.

"He's an acquaintance," I said coldly. Out of the corner of my eye, I saw Charlie's face fall just a little bit. But it was back to happy-go-lucky in an instant. I felt a little guilty for hurting his feelings. But as much as I liked Charlie, we just couldn't be friends, and I needed to let him know that one way or another.

Mom seemed to notice the discomfort and said, "So, are you staying for dinner?"

"No!" I said abruptly. They both blinked at me. "He was just here to help with homework," I rushed to explain. "And homework is done, so he was just leaving."

"Morgan, don't be rude," Mom chastised. Then she turned back to Charlie. "Would you like to stay?"

*No, no. Say no. Please say no*, I chanted over and over in my head.

"No, thank you, Mrs. Casey." Finally, he said something right for once! "My mom is probably wondering where I am, so I better go home. Can I take a rain check?"

"Of course." Mom smiled.

"Bye, Morgan."

"Bye," I said shortly.

Charlie let himself out.

When he was gone, Mom turned her stern gaze on me, silently scolding me for being so rude to my guest. As she walked away to start our dinner that we both knew Dad wouldn't bring home, I wondered if she would still be mad at me for treating Charlie the way I did if she knew my reasons behind it.

# Chapter 7

I had that same nightmare again that night. And again, I woke up screaming. The only difference this time was that I knew what was coming. After the initial terror had worn off, I lay in bed, thinking it all over. Twice now, Jamie had said, "They're coming." What was she talking about?

I rolled over onto my side.

I'd heard about dreams sometimes being visions of the future. I prayed that wasn't the case with this dream. If it was, I knew who was coming. And I knew what they wanted. And I knew they'd do anything to get it. They'd already proven that.

Paranoia set it. It was just a dream. But I was going to be extra careful from now on, just in case it was something more.

# Chapter 8

It was finally Friday. In my pre-Pennsylvania life, I would have been thrilled. My weekend would already be full of plans, plans, plans. And I wouldn't slow down until midnight Sunday night.

I was excited for no school; I'd give the weekend that. I was tired of homework and Charlie. But I was not ready for sitting around the house for two days straight.

I didn't really have a choice though. My new, overly cautious routine consisted of blending in even more than I had originally planned. Charlie hadn't been over since the night he helped me with homework, and I didn't talk to anyone for the rest of the week. That included Charlie. Maybe he finally got the message that I wasn't looking for a friend. I went to school, went home, ate dinner, did homework, and went to bed. It was like being grounded. But surprisingly, I didn't mind. I liked feeling safe.

With the school day over, I headed for my car. I stumbled through the parking lot, digging through my backpack, looking for my car keys and grumbling under my breath when I couldn't find them. I sighed and looked up when I got to my old, white Pontiac that didn't even look white anymore. I uselessly jerked on the door handle, not surprised when it didn't open.

"You might need these."

I jerked my head up to find Charlie standing on the passenger side of my car. He had his arms crossed on the roof and was swinging my keys on one of his fingers. I glared at him.

"Yeah, I might." I held out my hand, and Charlie tossed them to me. Pressing the unlock button, I opened the door and climbed in. Only to find that Charlie had done the exact same thing. "What are you doing?" I demanded.

Charlie shrugged. "Oh, nothing much. Sitting in your car."

I raised an eyebrow. "Why?"

Charlie looked off into space for a while, like he was thinking, and then shrugged again. "I dunno." He grinned. I didn't find this very funny.

"Get out."

"Why?" Charlie whined.

"Because I said so."

Charlie narrowed his eyes at me. "No," he said petulantly.

I gritted my teeth together and closed my eyes, taking a deep breath. Then I opened them again and looked him right in the eye.

"Get. Out. Of. My. Car."

"Can't I talk to you first?"

I took another deep breath. "Fine. Talk."

"I can be a jerk too, ya know."

"What's that supposed to mean?" I asked.

"Quit ignoring me. I mean, I get it if you don't like me. I'm fine with that. But you haven't told me to get lost yet. I'm trying to make you feel welcome and be your friend when you don't have any here, and you're making it very difficult. I could just choose to never even look at you again."

I let out a breath of air. "I'm sorry, okay?"

"You're really sorry?" Charlie was grinning again. It didn't surprise me that he couldn't be serious for more than five minutes. I smiled a little.

"Yeah, I'm really sorry. Can I go home now?" I started the car.

He ignored my question. "How sorry are you?"

"Very."

"Sorry enough to make it up to me?"

"Sure," I said noncommittally. Anything to get him out so I could go home.

"Come to the football game tonight."

Anything but that. I shook my head. "No, I can't. I …" I tried to think of an excuse as to why I couldn't go, but my mind drew a blank. I was completely and 100 percent plan-free.

"Come on, please. It'll be fun," Charlie begged. "It's the first game of the school year. Everyone goes. Plus, it'll make you feel like you belong."

Did I want to belong? I'd only been there a week, and I was already getting comfortable. A little too comfortable. I had let my guard down and let Charlie in. Now I was stuck with him. A thousand scenes played through my head. There were a lot of people at football games. How hard would it be for someone to come up and grab me, and then make a clean get away without anyone noticing until it was too late? Not hard enough.

I looked at Charlie, who was watching me mull over the situation. His eyes were expectant. I could tell he was excited for the game. Just like that, I knew he had me.

"Fine," I muttered. "I'll go."

Charlie smiled so wide I was afraid his cheeks would crack. "Okay. Don't forget. It starts at eight. I gotta go. Bye!" And with that, he was out of the car and jogging across the parking lot to his own car.

I shook my head in amusement and drove home, the danger of the football game in the back of my head.

# Chapter 9

Some say that when someone is kidnapped, and they can't remember anything about it, that's the most tragic part of the whole thing. They have no idea what happened to them or when or why. But I disagree with the people who say that. That's what I was thinking about as I worked my way through the thick crowd of people at the football game that night looking for Charlie. I think it's tragic when you can remember everything. You want to forget, but you can't, and you envy those people who can. Lost in my thoughts, I bumped into a group of teenagers. Seniors probably.

"Watch where you're going, kid," one guy growled. A couple of girls laughed at me. I stopped in my tracks to glare at them, hoping they would ask for an apology, just so I could refuse to give them one. But they were back to their own worlds and laughing like idiots within a couple of seconds, and I gave up staring them down. I stuffed my hands into my shorts pockets and kept walking, scanning for Charlie.

My practiced eyes finally fell on his smiling face. He was talking animatedly with a couple of middle-school kids. He threw his hands up in the air, and they laughed at whatever he said. Not wanting to interrupt, I stayed back, unseen in the crowd. At least until Charlie took a break from talking (amazing!) and looked around. When he saw me, he grinned and motioned for me to join him. Hesitantly, I complied.

"Guys," Charlie said to the kids, still grinning, "this is Morgan. She's new, so don't scare her off!" All five of them smiled a little and introduced themselves. I nodded politely and pretended that I would remember their names later, even though I knew I wouldn't.

One girl smiled at me. "Your hair is pretty," she said.

I smiled back a bit shyly. "Thanks." Self-conscious, I let my now chocolate brown hair fall over my eyes and wondered if she would have thought my old hair was pretty too.

After a few minutes of talking to them, Charlie said smoothly, "Okay, we'll leave you guys alone now." He looked around and then leaned closer to them like he was going to tell them a secret. "I'm sure you don't want to be seen with a couple high-school kids anyway. We're kind of lame." He stood up straight, wearing a triumphant smile when they all giggled. With a friendly wave, he started to walk away. I rushed to keep up.

"You're a class favorite," I observed.

Charlie shrugged. "I like kids," he said by way of explanation. "They're better than people our age. Everything was so simple then. Know what I mean?"

I nodded. "Maybe you like kids because you're like a kid yourself." I meant it to be kind of mean, so it would be an understatement to say that I was surprised when Charlie laughed.

"That's a good point," he said appreciatively. We kept walking around the field.

"So, is this all we're going to do?"

Charlie looked at me.

"I mean, seriously, this is stupid. Just walking around." I glanced at the scoreboard. "We're crushing these people. It's obvious they're not going to catch up. Can I go home now?"

"Nope." Charlie stopped walking. I stopped beside him. "This is what you do at a football game here. You walk around and talk to your friends and occasionally watch the game. What did you do at football games in—" He stopped suddenly, as if realizing he didn't know where I was from. I laughed and kept walking. Charlie jogged to catch up to me. "What's so funny?" he asked, a smile tugging at the corners of his mouth.

"Nothing. Just that you claim to be my friend, but you don't know a thing about me."

"I do too," Charlie defended himself.

"Okay." I stopped to face him and crossed my arms over my chest. "Name all the things you know about me."

"You have really, really dark brown hair." Charlie tugged at a piece of my hair playfully. "And cold, ice blue eyes that, frankly, are kind of freaky. You throw up at the sight of blood, you run away from cars, you're kind of antisocial, you're bad at science, a little clumsy, you have a mom and dad, looks like you're an only child." He screwed his mouth up in a weird way as he thought. Suddenly, he grabbed one of my wrists, undoing my crossed arms, and flipped my hand over, palm up. "And you have mysterious scars on your hands that I would like to know the backstory to."

I jerked my hand away and glowered at him. He had crossed the line when he mentioned my hands. I stuffed them in my pockets. "My hands are none of your business and you don't even know where I came from. So, technically, that means none of that other stuff matters." I started walking briskly. Suddenly, I didn't want to talk to Charlie anymore.

"So make it matter." Charlie followed me, completely oblivious to my anger. It irritated me that it was so easy for him and his long legs to keep up with me. "Tell me where you moved from."

I kept walking.

"Come on," Charlie pleaded. "Look, I'll make a deal with you. You tell me where you're from, and I'll tell you something about me."

I tried to will myself to keep walking and ignore him, but cursing my curiosity, I stopped to face him. "Deal."

Charlie raised one eyebrow, seemingly surprised that bribing me was so easy. "You first."

"I moved here from California. Your turn."

"I haven't lived here my whole life either. I moved from Texas."

I stared at him. That made absolutely no sense. "But ..."

Charlie held up a hand to stop me. "I know, I know. I don't have that famous southern drawl. I moved when I was twelve, so I've had a few years to get rid of it." He grinned, but I noticed that it wasn't a real Charlie grin. Actually, it seemed a little forced, which was totally out of character for Charlie. I dismissed it without question. "So, what were football games like back in California?"

I laughed a short laugh. "I have no idea. Never went to one."

"Why not?"

I shrugged. Again, we started walking. "I was too busy I guess. Lacrosse was practically my life. I ate, slept, and dreamt it. Every chance I got, I was practicing."

Charlie looked startled. "You play lacrosse?"

"Played," I corrected, suddenly quiet. I felt unease drop anchor in my stomach. I was openly talking about my past. I hadn't meant to mention lacrosse. I shouldn't have even told him where I was from. What if I accidently let something else slip? This conversation needed to end, and it needed to end now.

"Hey, are you all right?" Charlie asked, concern in his green eyes.

"No," I lied, feigning sick. "I don't feel good. Can I go home?"

"Yeah, of course," Charlie said, looking a little alarmed. "I'll make sure you get to your car okay."

I shook my head. "No, it's—"

"Please," Charlie interrupted. "If not for you, can I do it for me?" Wordlessly, I nodded, and we started for my car. I secretly felt safer walking in the darkening night with Charlie. It was better than walking by myself.

On our way to the car, Charlie ran right into the same group of teenagers I had earlier, jostling not only one, but two of them. I waited, ready for him to get yelled at or laughed at.

"Are you okay, Charlie? Sorry, man, that was my fault," said the guy who had told me to watch where I was going. I whirled around.

Charlie smiled tensely. "Yeah, it's okay."

The girls stared at him in admiration before we walked away.

"What was that all about?" I demanded.

Charlie pressed his mouth into a firm line. "Those kids are bad news, Morgan. You don't want to mess with them."

I rolled my eyes. "They just looked at you like you gave them eternal life or something, and you're telling me not to mess with them?"

"I've earned their respect," Charlie explained vaguely. "They think we're friends, and I still don't want to get on their bad side. Trust me, okay?"

I nodded and didn't press further. This other side of Charlie chilled me. Finally, we were at my car. I slid into the driver's seat and turned the key. Nothing happened. I flipped the car back off and then turned it on again. Nothing. Again. Nothing happened. With a sigh, I got back out and looked at Charlie, who was watching inquisitively.

"It won't start," I said in exasperation.

"Way to point out the obvious." Charlie grinned as he teased me. I stuck my tongue out at him, and he chuckled. I watched as he popped the hood and his head disappeared under it. It only took a few minutes for him to emerge again with a confused look on his face.

"No wonder it won't start. Your spark plugs are missing. You did drive this here, right?"

"No," I rolled my eyes, "I pulled it the whole way here with a rope! Of course I drove it here!"

Charlie held up his hands, as if trying to stop me from attacking him. "Just making sure. Jeez. Then how'd they go missing?"

"Someone took them out?" I suggested, feeling the uneasiness again. It was getting way too familiar.

"It was probably just some stupid prank," Charlie said dismissively. "No big deal. Here, I'll drive you home."

Realizing I didn't have any other choice when it came to a way to get home, I reluctantly followed Charlie to his car.

# Chapter 10

Charlie drove well under the speed limit on the way to my house. It was agonizingly slow. This ride was better than any of the others though. It wasn't quiet. Charlie had the radio on. Popular music that I didn't care about enough to know hummed in the background. Charlie hummed with it.

"So, do you miss it?" Charlie asked suddenly.

I inaudibly sighed. I had been enjoying the period of no conversation.

"Miss what?"

Charlie shrugged. "You know. California."

I shook my head and whispered, "No."

"Why not? I mean you only lived there for your whole life."

I glared at him. "Why do you insist on knowing all my business?"

Charlie grinned. All I got as an answer was a shrug.

After a couple seconds of silence, I asked, "Do you miss Texas?"

Charlie was quiet for a long time. "No," he said. His face clouded over. His eyes went dark.

"Why not?" I mocked. He didn't notice it.

"I have my reasons."

Now I was really intrigued. "And they are?" I prodded.

Charlie smiled faintly. "You don't need to know."

I punched him in the arm. "Tell me."

He laughed. "Was that supposed to hurt?"

"No! Now tell me!" Then as an afterthought, I added, "Please."

Charlie shook his head, still smiling a little, and pulled the car to the side of the road. He stabbed the power button on the radio with his finger, and suddenly the car was eerily silent. "How about we make a deal: I'll tell you everything about me as long as you promise to tell me everything, and I mean everything, about you. Deal?" He stuck out his hand.

"What do you mean by 'everything'?" I asked skeptically.

Charlie did that funny thing with his mouth again. "You can ask me whatever questions you want, and I'll answer them truthfully and I can do the same. Okay?"

Before I realized I was doing it, I nodded and said, "Deal."

"You have to shake on it," Charlie insisted.

I shook my head. "Do you want to keep this deal or not?"

"Fine." He took his hand back.

"I get to ask you first."

A bit hesitantly, Charlie nodded.

"Okay, why don't you miss Texas?"

"It's a long story."

"I've got time."

Charlie settled back in his seat. "I, umm, I wasn't really a good kid."

I found that hard to believe.

"I mean, I was until I turned ten," Charlie continued. "But a couple months before my tenth birthday, my dad walked out on us."

"Us being … ?" I asked.

"Me, my mom, and my little sister, Jenny. Even now, none of us really know why he left. He just … did. Anyway, I was really mad at … everyone, I guess. I ditched all my old friends and got new ones. They were nothing like me or my old friends. They were the kids who spent their days in the principal's office and constantly got in trouble. They talked me into doing things I never would have even thought about doing before."

I didn't ask. I could tell he didn't want me to.

"So, I spent around two years getting into trouble. And school was getting really hard. So on my twelfth birthday, I dropped out and ran away from home. I did a lot of bad things the couple weeks I lived on the streets. I stole things to stay alive, and I stole things for the fun of it. Needless to say, the police caught up to me and brought me back home. With a record that will never go away. That's when Mom made me see a shrink. After a couple months of that, I wanted a new start. I didn't want to go back to school and hear the whispers. So we just moved. I like it here because no one has ever heard of me. I ruined my life there. But I got a new start here." He took a deep breath and closed his eyes. His hands were fists on his lap. The pain of remembering was etched into his normally smiling face.

I waited in silence. After what seemed like a long time, he finally opened his eyes. He was smiling again.

"Any more questions?"

I shook my head slowly, shocked into silence. I wanted to comfort him somehow. When I lived in California, comforting people had been an instinct. Second nature because I did it so often. I couldn't remember how anymore. It had been too long.

"Then ... my turn?" Charlie asked.

A streak of panic flashed through me. Was I ready to talk about it yet? I took a deep breath and tried to trick myself into thinking there was a sense of calm washing over me that I didn't feel. I had to be ready. A deal's a deal.

"Yeah. Ask away," I allowed.

"Why don't you miss California? Why do you keep to yourself the way you do?" For the second time that night, he grabbed my wrist and flipped it over, tracing the puffy, pink scar tissue pointedly with his eyes, and just asked: "Why?"

Slowly, carefully, I pulled my hand back and balled them into fists. A thousand comebacks for each and every one of

Charlie's nosy questions crossed my mind. But I forced myself into forming the answers and making them come off my lips.

I smiled. But it was a grim smile. The kind that holds no humor. "All the answers, they're tied together somehow."

"That makes it easier then." Charlie grinned and looked at me expectantly.

"My story is long too," I warned him. It was only fair.

He gave me a look that said, "It's okay."

I took a deep breath and let the memories I'd been trying to hide from for so long flood back all at once. "I had a best friend. Her name was Jamie, and we'd been friends since before I can remember. We were the kind of friends who told each other, very literally, everything. From what I can remember, we only fought twice. And they were little fights. The ones that last maybe an hour or two of not talking, and then we were better." I could tell him an endless amount of Jamie stories, but it would be over faster if I just cut to the chase. "When we were fourteen, both Jamie's parents lost their jobs. Times were really tough for her family. They were all desperate for money."

I remembered how Jamie would always be scrounging up extra time to study so she could graduate early and get a job. Then when she wasn't studying, she was either taking care of her younger siblings or holding down at least three or four part-time jobs all at once, just to help out. But I didn't feel the need to include that. Charlie didn't need to know all of Jamie's business.

"Anyway, I guess things eventually got easier. But I didn't know how. Both Jamie's parents were still out of work, and Jamie was even busier than before. She would be really secretive. Like, before, she would always tell me she was going to work at whatever mini-mart or convenience store she had to be at that day. But she stopped doing that and just started disappearing for hours with no explanation."

Charlie nodded, signaling to me that he was listening attentively. That part of the story had been easy. I took a deep breath and closed my eyes for a second, bracing myself for the hard part coming.

"Finally, she had a night off, and she spent the night."

I would never forget that moment when Jamie told me where she was getting the extra money. It was permanently carved into my memory, haunting me forever.

"I kept hounding her about it ..."

I remember yelling at her. *Friends don't keep secrets!* That was how I got her to tell, by saying it over and over and over.

"Until finally she told me." I was choking on my words, trying to get them out in a way that made sense. "She met with some people who wanted information that she could get. It was information about some other country—Russia, I think. I guess her dad had kind of worked in politics and had all this stuff on a special computer."

I almost wanted to smile as I remembered Jamie and her computer skills. She could hack any type you set in front of her.

"They gave her money, like a lot of money, just to say that she would. Then they gave her even more when she came through for them."

"Who were they?" Charlie asked, his eyes round with curiosity.

"When she asked, they said they weren't from the government or anything. Just a group of people who were angry at Russia for something."

She never told me what group, and I never asked. I was too shell-shocked.

"I ... I told her to stop. Something in my gut told me there would be consequences. But she didn't listen to me. Her, secret trading I guess you could call it, went on for a year. And she told me everything that she told the group she was selling the secrets to. So I knew everything they did."

"Why isn't it still going on?" Charlie whispered.

It felt like he punched me repeatedly in the stomach. I tried a bunch of different words out in my head, but nothing sounded right. Charlie was just going to have to deal with my jumbled thoughts.

"They—Russia, I guess—caught wind of it and sent some spies over here. They ... they took me first and tried to get me to tell them what I knew." The words were coming out fast. There was no stopping them now. "I, I don't know. I was stupid and stubborn and refused to tell them anything. That's when they got Jamie too."

Everything that had happened flashed in front of my eyes.

"She wouldn't tell them either." I held my fists at my chest, like I was protecting my hands. "They ... Charlie, they blindfolded me and took a knife ..."

I tasted something terrible in the back of my throat. I felt like I needed to puke.

"I ... I think they had it in fire first. So it would be hot. And it was really dull. And they traced my lifelines with it."

My hands were on fire. I felt the blade going over my lifelines again. It hurt so much. I felt a scream rise in my chest and forced it down again, trying to remind myself that I was here in the car. Not back where my nightmares thrive.

"I guess they were hoping to get me to talk. They did both hands slowly. Then when I was still quiet, they argued and left." I made my breathing as even as possible. "Jamie wouldn't say anything either, and they must have thought I was the weaker one, so they focused on me. A few days after," I looked at my hands, "they brought Jamie in and threatened to kill her if I didn't tell them everything I knew. I didn't believe them." I whispered the last part.

I was ashamed to admit it. I thought it would be like the movies. The bad guys would chicken out and leave her alone. It was my bullheaded stupidity that killed her.

"Charlie, they killed her right in front of me!" I screamed, wishing it wasn't true, that I could yell, "Gotcha!" I couldn't though, and it wasn't fair.

I was back in the basement. Just like it was happening all over again. I saw Jamie tied to a chair across the room from me. I saw her mouth: *It'll be okay.* And I saw the tears in her eyes right before they pulled the trigger.

"I blacked out after that. According to Mom and Dad, someone driving by heard the gunshot and called the police. I was rescued only a half hour after that."

I rested my hands on my lap and stared at them, wishing I'd never even gone to the stupid football game. Charlie was quiet for such a long time I thought he fell asleep. I looked at him. He was staring out the windshield.

Finally he muttered, "Oh my God." He looked at me. Then, "Oh my God." Like that was the only phrase he remembered how to say. "I'm so sorry, Morgan. If I'd have known ... I'm sorry. And I thought I'd been through a lot."

"I know," I whispered, sounding heartbroken even to myself. "It's just not fair." Eleven days. I was held captive for eleven days.

Charlie stared at me. "Please," he begged. "Please don't cry."

"I'm not crying," I said irritably. Charlie reached over, wiped my cheek, and then held out his fingers. A single lonely teardrop was trapped on his thumb. I hurriedly wiped my eyes with my sweatshirt sleeves and forced any other tears back. I hadn't cried since we moved, and I wasn't planning on starting again.

"I ... Morgan, I know this may be hard to believe," Charlie awkwardly stumbled under his own words. "But things, well they definitely aren't okay, but they're better than what they used to be. I mean, those spy guys or whatever they were, they can't hurt you or anyone else anymore. The police got them."

I didn't say a word.

"Right?" Charlie nervously asked. "They did get them, right?"

Again, I kept my mouth shut. Charlie waited several long seconds for my confirmation. It was never going to come.

"Morgan?" he asked. "Is there something else?" I could practically see the wheels turning in his head. He had to be thinking about my secrecy, how I was so quiet, how I didn't want friends, and how apprehensive I was around people. Then, I silently watched as he came to a dark conclusion.

I allowed him his out by saying, "No, Charlie, they … the spies escaped."

His lips parted in surprise. I rested my head on the cool window and closed my eyes, finally facing reality: I still wasn't safe.

"Can you take me home now?" I asked. Wordlessly, Charlie put the car into drive and pulled back onto the road. I was emotionally drained, and I let my thoughts wander, letting myself think about anything other than my sinister past.

# Chapter 11

The night had turned inky black by the time Charlie and I got back to my house. He carefully pulled up to the sidewalk to let me out. Resting my hand on the door handle, I looked at him.

"I'm really sorry about your dad," I said quietly. "He doesn't know what he's missing."

Charlie looked hard at the steering wheel and then up at me. A sad smile teased the corners of his mouth. "Thanks."

I just looked at him for a few seconds because I had never heard someone say it like that before. He sounded so genuine. I nodded and popped the car door open. As I walked up to my house, I noticed all the lights were still on. My parents were still up. I opened the door and let it quietly snap shut behind me. I slipped off my sneakers and padded into the living room. Dad's angry voice made me stop in my tracks at the doorway.

"You let her go out?" he shouted.

They were sitting on opposite ends of the couch, as far apart as possible with the TV on mute.

I could tell by the tone of her voice that Mom was trying to keep her cool, but it wasn't working. "She's finally trying to live a normal life again. We can't deny her that."

"We can if it's the only way to keep her safe!"

"She is safe, Ben! If you haven't noticed, we moved to the middle of nowhere!"

"She should've gone into the Witness Protection Program," Dad grumbled.

"What would they have done?" Mom screamed. "Given her a different name and shipped her off somewhere without us?

She'd still be in the same situation she is now—only without her parents!"

Dad fell silent. I leaned forward, hoping to be able to hear if he decided on something to say. A floorboard creaked in protest against the sudden shift of my weight. Mom and Dad jumped and turned around. I sighed and pretended I had just come in. If Dad had been going to reply, he wasn't going to now.

I walked over and sat between them. I dug my hand in between the couch cushions and retrieved the remote, pushing the mute button again. Sound blared from the TV. A few commercials about crappy deals and a new restaurant opening went by before I was ready to get out of the tense atmosphere.

Mom was the first one to speak up when she saw me start for my bedroom.

"How was the ...?"

"Football game," I supplied impatiently. "It was fine."

"Did you make any friends there?"

I resisted the urge to roll my eyes. Again with the friends thing. Why did she have to be so insistent about me making friends?

"No."

"Was Charlie there?"

"Yeah ..." I made it sound more like a question than an answer.

"Did you talk to him at all?"

I thought about lying but decided there was no point. "Yeah."

Mom nodded thoughtfully, looking pleased. "Okay," she said. "Okay."

Dad remained pouting, staring at the TV screen. I stuffed my hands into my pockets and went upstairs without another word.

I don't know how long I'd been lying in bed before I heard a knock on the door. Puzzled, I sat up.

"Um, come in?"

The door creaked on its hinges when Mom opened it. For a while, we just looked at each other. She'd only been in my room a few times, and she never stayed long. I expected her to ask me if I knew where we packed the candles or something irrelevant like that, so I was shocked into silence when she came over and sat on my bed.

"You got home sooner than you want us to think, didn't you?" she finally asked.

"What do you mean?" I asked, pretending to sound completely confused.

"Morgan," Mom warned. Something inside me snapped. She hadn't sounded like that, sounded like a mom, since the day before I was taken.

"I got home in time to hear you guys fighting," I admitted.

"I'm sorry you had to hear it," Mom whispered.

I shook my head, my eyes closed.

"I'm used to it." I opened my eyes to see the look of pain cross her face. Instead of the triumph I was expecting to feel from hurting her feelings, I felt guilt.

"You've heard us before." It wasn't a question. She knew that I had but wanted my confirmation.

"Every night."

She brought her hand up to stroke my hair. "I'm sorry," she said again.

I said, "I know." Because I did.

"Your dad and I have totally different views on what's going to keep you safe and happy. But we both want those things for you, so I guess it doesn't really matter how you get them. We love you, Morgan."

I studied my bedspread. "I love you guys too. I just wish I wasn't the reason you're fighting."

Mom didn't have anything to say to that. We both knew it was true. I was the reason my normally loving parents went to bed angry at each other every night.

"Things are going to get better," Mom promised.

I smiled, but it was a little one. "Okay." I wanted to believe her. I really did. But it seemed so far from the truth, I just couldn't. We sat in silence for a few minutes. Mom watched me closely, and I kept my head ducked.

Finally she asked, "How are you doing, Morgan?"

"Charlie knows." I was avoiding the question.

"Charlie knows ..." She sounded confused, like she wanted to ask me what Charlie knew. Then it dawned on her. "Oh. How?"

I sat on my hands, just because I didn't want to look at them. Every time I talked about it, they hurt. "I told him. Tonight."

I waited, ready for the disappointed look. The words she would yell to let me know I'd made a mistake. How she thought we agreed I would tell no one. But it didn't come. She didn't even ask for an explanation, and I was grateful because I didn't even know why I told him. I just ... did.

Mom looked thoughtful. "He seems like a good kid," she finally said. "You should give him a chance."

"I'll try," I lied. Charlie and I being friends wasn't likely.

"So how are you?" Mom asked again.

"Fine," I said. "I'm just fine, Mom."

She looked relieved as she drew me to her for a hug. I rested my head on her shoulder and felt her gently rubbing my back.

"Mom?" I asked.

"What, Morgan?"

"Can I sleep with you and Dad tonight?"

Her hand didn't even stop tracing circles on my back. Instead of being surprised at my childish request, she just said, "Are you ready to go to bed now or do you want to sit and talk for a little bit more?"

So we went to her and Dad's room where Dad was already under the blankets watching TV. He didn't say anything when Mom lay down and I crawled in between them, just kissed the top of my head.

The bed wasn't very big, and it definitely wasn't meant for three people to sleep in, but somehow we made it work.

I thought about how I had answered Mom when she asked me if I was okay. It had just been another lie. The truth was I was scared. But, sandwiched between my parents, I couldn't fight sleep for very long.

# Chapter 12

I opened my eyes and realized I wasn't in my mom and dad's bed. I wasn't even in my house. The cement floor under me was cold. I was cold. I pushed myself into a sitting position and looked around. A basement with cement blocks for walls and no windows. One door at the top of a long flight of stairs.

I felt the weight of dread in my stomach. I knew where I was, and I knew what was going to happen. This was one of those dreams where you know you're dreaming, but you're still afraid of what's to come.

I looked around, expecting to see Jamie, just like in all the other dreams. But she wasn't there. I was alone.

I stood up and started to look around some more, but a brick wall suddenly appeared out of nowhere and caused me to jump back, fall, and land on my butt. I watched as, one by one and starting at the top, bricks started to fall. I scooted back to dodge them. They landed hard on the cement and cracked so that rebuilding the wall wasn't an option.

Bricks kept falling, eventually revealing people I knew too well. People I never wanted to see again.

There were three of them. One holding a chain and a blindfold. One resting his hands on the back of a metal chair. One with a dull knife covered in the dark stains of blood. All smirking smugly at me.

Beside them stood Jamie with her hands and feet bound together and a gag in her mouth. She was pale, and her eyes showed panic.

The wall kept coming down, and with each brick that fell, the four took a step closer—until there was finally just nothing there to stop them.

# Chapter 13

I bolted upright, breathing hard, and looked around. I saw the familiar pattern of my parents' flowered wallpaper, saw the dark hardwood floor and the small, outdated TV sitting on the dresser, and took a deep breath. I was back.

I heard pans banging and the shuffling of feet coming from downstairs, accompanied by the smell of French toast. I slid out of bed and stumbled toward the bathroom. Placing my hands on the sink and leaning forward, I took a long look at myself in the mirror. The nightmare had left my face pale and my eyes transparent. My hair was a mess, and my vision was blurred from still being groggy.

Frowning, I pushed myself away from the sink and got in the shower, turning the water as hot as I could stand it. I sighed and tipped my head back, letting the burning water run over my head and down my back, leaving trails of red on my skin. I wouldn't let myself think about the nightmare, or how it was different from all the other ones I'd had.

I just stood under the water until the room was hot and stuffy and full of steam. I turned the water off, stepped out of the shower, and wrapped myself in a towel. Then I walked back to the mirror and wiped the condensation from the glass, pleased to see that color had returned to my cheeks.

I tiptoed into my room and shut the door behind me before pulling on light-colored jean shorts, a dark-blue T-shirt, and socks that had one too many holes in them.

When I got downstairs, Dad was sitting at the table, writing furiously on an official looking piece of paper, and Mom was standing at the oven, busily dunking pieces of bread into an eggy mixture and then carefully placing them in a pan. I took a seat opposite Dad and watched them navigate in their own little worlds. It was only when Mom set the first stack of French toast on the table that they noticed me.

"Good morning," she said brightly, handing me a plate and a fork.

"Morning," I mumbled.

Dad looked up and smiled at me. "How'd you sleep?"

"Fine." I reached for two pieces of French toast and dropped them on my plate before smothering them with butter and syrup. Looking at my breakfast, my mouth started to water. The bread was visibly moist from the syrup. Some sections were colorless from the egg, and other parts, my favorite parts, were dark from the cinnamon. Hungrily, I picked up my fork and dug in, closing my eyes in bliss as my favorite breakfast food practically dissolved in my mouth. The only noise in the kitchen was an occasional fork scraping a plate.

I looked up just in time to see Dad with his mouth open, about to say something. The phone rang. I jumped up to answer it. Dad's eyes fell.

"Hello?"

"Morgan?"

"Charlie?"

Charlie laughed. "Yeah, it's me. I was afraid I got the wrong number."

"How did you get my number?"

"Phonebook," Charlie said.

"Our phone number is in the phonebook?" I asked dumbly.

Charlie laughed again. "Didn't I just say that? Is it a little early for you or something?"

"No," I said defensively. "Did you call just to make fun of me or do you want something?"

"What are you doing today?"

I shrugged, forgetting for a moment that he couldn't see me. "Nothing that I know of. Why?"

"I have to take my sister to get her hair cut. You want to come?"

"No."

"Why not?" Charlie sounded disappointed. I was happy that I couldn't see the expression that went with it.

"I just don't want to." Actually, I kind of did want to. It was better than staying in the house all day. But it wasn't safe.

"I'll come get you in ten minutes."

"But, Charlie, I don't—" The dial tone in my ear let me know that I was now talking to myself. I was irritated when I hung up the phone. Charlie was relentless.

"I'm going out in ten minutes," I informed Mom and Dad. They had their heads bent over their breakfast. I had to give them credit; they were at least pretending they hadn't been listening.

Something in Dad's eyes changed. Mom looked happy. Grudgingly, Dad reached into his pocket and then handed me a couple bills and a lot of quarters.

"Be careful," he said. Then, pointing to the quarters, added, "Call us if anything—" He coughed uncomfortably. "Call us if you need anything."

Mom shot him a looked that clearly said: *Nice save.*

"I will," I promised. But I wasn't sure I could. I hadn't seen a single pay phone anywhere in town, and since the FBI made us get rid of all our cell phones, I didn't have a way to stay in contact with my parents.

A car horn beeped from out front.

"Bye." I headed for the door.

"Have fun!" Mom called after me. I pushed the screen door open and walked out to where Charlie was waiting.

"Hey," he said when I was in the passenger seat.

"Hi," I said coldly.

He chuckled and shook his head at me. I scowled at him in return.

He turned around in his seat. "Morgan, that's Jenny. Jenny, this is my friend, Morgan."

I turned around too. Buckled up in the backseat was a small girl with honey-blonde hair, so much like Charlie's, and brown doe-like eyes.

"Hi, Morgan!" she said excitedly. I couldn't help but smile a little.

"Hi, Jenny."

She giggled when I said her name. I turned back around in my seat as Charlie started driving.

"How old are you?" Jenny asked me.

"Sixteen."

I heard her sigh dramatically. "I wish I was sixteen like you and Charlie. I want to drive!"

I laughed and looked at Charlie. He was smiling. This was a new smile. I couldn't read the emotion behind it.

"She's wanted to drive since I got my license. I let her steer in the yard sometimes, but it just isn't enough, is it Jenny?" He took his eyes off the road long enough to look at her in the mirror.

I turned around again so I could see her. She shook her head adamantly. "I want to make it go!"

Charlie laughed. I turned to face the front. A few seconds later, I felt someone tapping my arm. For the third time in five minutes, I turned around.

"Want to know how old I am?" Jenny asked me.

"Sure."

"I'm five and three quarters. That means I'll be six soon." She sounded so proud. I smiled, knowing how much of that pride had to do with the "and three quarters" part.

"When's your birthday?" I asked.

She looked up toward the roof of the car, as if the answer was written there. After a few seconds, she said, "October fourth."

I looked at the floor, thinking for a second until it came to me. I looked at her again. "That means your birthstone is opal."

She scrunched up her eye brows, making a comical puzzled face. "What's that?"

"It's a stone that's white with flecks of different colors in it. If you hold it up to another color, it will become mostly that color. It's really pretty," I assured her.

Jenny's eyes grew as wide as saucers. "Wow." She looked completely awed. Smiling, I turned back around.

A few minutes later, we pulled up to a building that said Classic Kid's Barber Shop.

"We're here," Charlie needlessly announced. He put the car into park and got out. I followed his lead. We waited for Jenny to get out, and when she did, she took Charlie's hand and we walked inside.

I was a bit taken aback by what I saw. The first thing I noticed was that there were no chairs. Instead, there were animals that looked like they came from a carousel all lined up for kids to sit on. To my right was a waiting room full of plastic balls and blocks and chalkboards. I wondered how often the room got used. We were the only ones in the shop as far as I could see. The whole shop was painted with vibrant yellows and greens and blues. It looked out of place. Like it belonged in a movie and not in our bland little world.

Shortly after entering, a short man with graying hair and an easy, contagious smile greeted us. I melted into the background. He shook Charlie's hand.

"Nice to see you again, Charlie." Then he bent down to Jenny's level and said, "How are you today, Ms. Ames?"

Jenny giggled, clearly pleased to be treated like an adult. "Good."

The man stood up, smiling the whole time. "Good. Now who's getting their hair cut today?" he teased. His eyes scanned first Charlie, and then Jenny, before finally resting on me. "I'll be right with you."

"No, it's okay. She's with us," Charlie said.

"Well, in that case, my name's Jerry." He outstretched his hand, but Charlie pushed his arm down, telling Jerry something with his eyes that I couldn't understand.

"Morgan," I said quietly.

"Are you helping Charlie babysit?" he asked, the smile never leaving his face. In a way, he reminded me of Charlie.

"I guess so." I didn't bother to add that I was dragged along.

"Okay. Well, Jenny, I guess it's time to cut some of that hair."

Jenny raced for a horse and climbed on. "I want it to here," she told him, pointing to her arm a few inches below her shoulder.

Jerry nodded and started cutting. It didn't take him long, seeing how her hair was maybe only half an inch below where she wanted it. Before I knew it, Charlie was handing Jerry a few bills and we were leaving.

Back in the car, Charlie counted how much money he had left, smiling when he was done.

"How does ice cream sound?"

Jenny squealed with delight. Charlie laughed.

"I'm going to take that as a 'yes.' How about you, Morgan? Want to go for ice cream?"

I shrugged. "I might as well. I'm already in the car, aren't I?"

Soon we were all sitting at a wooden table outside an ice-cream shop. Jenny's face was already covered in chocolate, and I was certain there was more ice cream on her than in her, even though Charlie made her get a bowl instead of a cone like she originally wanted. As he tried to keep up with cleaning Jenny's mess, Charlie's strawberry ice cream was slowly melting. The pale-pink sweet grew soft and leisurely rolled down the cone, settling on the scarred wood and making a small puddle.

Watching them, I licked my own vanilla ice cream thoughtfully. Charlie smiled that smile again as he wiped her mouth. It was a tender smile, I decided, the kind that you got from your grandparents. The kind that said, "I love you." I couldn't help but smile too, seeing how close they were. Jenny's hero-worship was just as apparent as Charlie's irrevocable devotion. It was a nice, warm feeling to be around them.

And it masked the feeling of being watched that lurked inside me.

# Chapter 14

Anxious, I checked the rearview mirror. My anxiety doubled. I nervously fidgeted with a loose thread on the bottom of my shirt and peeked at the mirror again.

"Charlie?" I whispered. Charlie glanced at me, taking his eyes off the road for only a second or two. We'd been driving again for a good ten minutes now.

"Why are you whispering?" There was laughter in his voice.

"Because I don't want to scare your sister." That got his attention.

"What's wrong?" He was whispering now too. Urgency replaced the laughter.

I jerked my thumb over my shoulder. "Do you recognize that car?" I asked, almost afraid of what I knew the answer would be.

Charlie's eyes flitted to the rearview mirror.

"No." His hands tightened on the steering wheel. His knuckles were white. "Do you?" he asked hesitantly.

"No." But I knew I wouldn't. They wouldn't keep the same car. They were smarter than that. I turned around in my seat slightly to see if I could see any faces in the windshield of the car behind us, catching out of the corner of my eye that Jenny was sound asleep in her car seat. *Good,* I thought, *she doesn't need any of this.* I focused on the windshield, but I couldn't see a thing. Tinted windows. Why would an SUV have tinted windows? I faced the front again.

"Who is it?" Charlie was tense; that much was obvious.

I shook my head. "I don't know. The windows are too dark. But they've been following us since we left the ice-cream shop."

"Do you think it's ... you know ... them?"

"No," I said immediately.

"Bull."

I slumped my shoulders in defeat. It was too easy for Charlie to see right through my lie. "I really don't know."

Suddenly, Charlie floored the gas pedal and turned sharply to the left onto a street completely empty of cars, but not lacking in homes. I instinctively grabbed the restriction handle on the roof of the car. "Better safe than sorry," he said through clenched teeth.

I looked back; the SUV gained some speed but kept a good distance behind us. Charlie accelerated the car a little more. The SUV accelerated a little more. I turned around and laid my head back with my eyes closed, trying to calm my breathing and keep the panic at bay.

Charlie swore under his breath. I opened my eyes, and my stomach dropped. I read the sign ahead of us again. Dead end. *Dead is right,* I thought sourly. My grip on the handle grew tighter. Next thing I knew, Charlie was taking another sharp turn and pulling into an empty driveway. He put the car in park and switched it off. We waited. The SUV cruised by, pulled into another driveway right across the street, backed out, and casually drove away. The license plate, I noticed, was caked with mud. We sat there, breathing hard, lost in our own thoughts, until Charlie broke the silence.

"Well, that was just about the fastest car chase I've ever been in." He was grinning, but it didn't reach his eyes. His green irises were full of concern as he stared at me.

I squinted at him. "You've been in a car chase before?"

"Nope." He twisted the ignition and put the car in reverse, looking over his shoulder to back out of the driveway. "That's why it was the fastest one I've ever been in."

I laughed. I actually laughed. And when Charlie heard it, his grin reached his eyes.

Slowly, I let go of the handle, finding it a bit painful because my fingers had cramped up. I looked back to check on Jenny and smiled when I saw her head lolled to the side. She was still fast asleep. That's when I noticed the direction Charlie was going.

"This isn't the way to my house," I objected.

"I know. My mom should be home from work. We're going to my place."

I wanted to argue and demand that he take me home, but I didn't. He had that concerned look back in his eyes.

# Chapter 15

Before I knew it, Charlie was leading me into a small, one-story, brick house surrounded by lush green shrubs and a perfectly manicured lawn. In one arm, he cradled a still sleeping Jenny. With his other hand, he grasped my wrist, carefully avoiding my hand.

A beautiful woman who looked to be in her midforties met us at the door. I studied her before approaching, a habit I had picked up in the last year or so. Her brown eyes were cautious, letting everyone who saw her know that she had seen a lot and overcome even more. Her hair was probably very blonde at one point, but aging was starting to make it turn slightly gray. She wore messy jeans and a simple T-shirt that had just about come to its end.

"She fell asleep after ice cream," Charlie said, gently passing Jenny to her. The woman gave Charlie a mock frown. "You spoil her," she said in a soft voice.

Charlie just grinned. Then he turned to me. "Mom, this is my friend, Morgan." He let go of my wrist. I rubbed my arm shyly.

"Hi," I murmured.

"Hello, Morgan. You can call me Susan. Or Suzie if you like, it really doesn't matter to me." The next thing I knew, Charlie's mom was hugging me with one arm, awkwardly squishing Jenny between us. By the time I got over the shock enough to hug her back, she had already pulled away. "Well, I guess Jenny should go lie down. I'll talk to you later." She shot me a smile, showing off a perfect row of pearly white teeth, and Charlie kissed her cheek before she disappeared inside.

I sat down on the steps.

"We can go inside too," Charlie informed me.

"I'm not staying. I still don't know why I let you bring me here in the first place. So you're gonna do whatever you think you need to do, and then you're taking me home."

Charlie sat down on the steps next to me. "I was planning on taking you home eventually," he defended himself. "It's not like I'm going to hold you hostage or anything."

I involuntarily cringed.

"Sorry," he said.

I waved my hand dismissively. "Whatever. Why exactly did you bring me here?"

"You think it was them, don't you?"

I frowned at him. "Way to be subtle," I said sarcastically.

He shrugged. "Don't you?"

I studied the back of my hands and sighed in exasperation. "I don't know, Charlie. I really don't. If I think it's them, then I could just be paranoid. But if I don't think it's them, then I could be in denial. I'm not sure what to think. Why can't you just leave me alone about it?"

"Because I need to know how careful we have to be from now on."

"We?" I arched an eyebrow at him. He nodded emphatically. "Since when did my problems become our problems?"

"Since I saw how scared you were back there." Charlie gazed at me intensely, studying my reaction.

I rolled my eyes. "I was not scared," I scoffed.

Charlie smiled crookedly at me. "Weren't you? Because you sure looked it to me."

I playfully punched him in the arm. "Yeah, just keep telling yourself that."

"What are you going to do?" He was suddenly serious again.

I shrugged and hugged my arms around myself self-consciously. "I don't know. Stay in more, I guess. Just in case. You know?"

"How about giving the FBI a call?" Charlie suggested.

"And tell them what? That a car followed us for a few minutes and then turned around when we appeared to be arriving home? They won't care."

"Well, at least tell them the make and model of the car. I know we don't have a license number to give them. But you said the windows were tinted, right?" I nodded. "Well, you can tell them that too. Just to keep them updated. Let them know you're concerned, all right?"

"Why should I?"

Charlie paused, carefully considering his answer. "It will make me feel better."

I gave him a chilly look. "You're too overprotective." It came out nicer than I meant it to.

"Some people consider that a good quality." Charlie laughed. I didn't really see what there was to laugh about. I stood up and wiped my shorts off.

"Not people who just want to be left alone. You promised you'd take me home," I said impatiently. "Let's go."

"Fine." Charlie got up, and we got back in the car.

"I can't wait until I get my car back," I grumbled under my breath as I fastened my seatbelt. Charlie laughed again.

"I called a mechanic after I dropped you off last night. You should get it back in time to drive yourself to and from school, no worries."

I looked at him, startled. I hadn't thought of calling a mechanic. Charlie caught my eye.

"What?" he asked, clearly amused. "Did you think your car was going to fix itself?"

"No," I said defensively. "I just didn't think you would call a mechanic for me." I hesitated. "Thanks."

Charlie smiled, pleased with himself. "Don't mention it."

Soon, but not soon enough, Charlie was letting me out in front of my house. I was just about to shut the car door when Charlie's voice stopped me.

"Hey," he said.

"What?"

"Don't worry too much about today. The car thing. It's probably nothing."

"Why do I get the feeling you're more worried about it than I am?"

Charlie grinned his signature grin and shrugged. "No clue."

I leaned heavily on the car door. "Either way, I'll call the FBI tomorrow, just because I know it will bug them."

Charlie chuckled. "Atta girl. Well, I guess I'll see you tomorrow."

"See me tomorrow?" I asked, straightening up. "Wha—?" But Charlie, smiling to himself, had already reached over and slammed the door closed before I could finish. With one last friendly wave, he drove away.

I threw my hands up and gave a loud cry of frustration as I stomped into the house.

# Chapter 16

There are some things you can force yourself to forget. You can go all day without it ever crossing your mind. You can think you've escaped it. But the truth is, you can never escape it. In the dark, early hours of the morning, it finds you. I learned that the morning after my day with Charlie and his sister.

I rolled over onto my side. The luminescent light on the clock face mocked me: 2:14 a.m. Why was I awake? I thought back to the night before, remembering how I wasn't hungry for dinner (thanks to Charlie buying me ice cream) and how I had escaped to my room without a word to Mom or Dad. Surprisingly, sleep had come easily, and no nightmares had invaded. So I was back to my question.

Why was I awake?

I rolled back over so I didn't have to stare at the clock. Instead, I watched shadows dance on the wall. The floor. The ceiling.

A car passed the house. I listened as the faint roar of the engine drove by and slowly faded. There was only silence again.

Unfortunately, with the silence came bad memories I'd been trying so hard to keep buried.

"Come on, I'll race you!" And Jamie took off across the street.

I took the time to call, "Cheater!" before sprinting after her. From what I could tell, she ran into the woods and I knew she was following the trail we made when we were nine. Hard to believe it was only five years ago.

When I finally caught up to her, she was sitting on a log beside a small stream and poking the water thoughtfully with a stick.

"You so cheated," I said, coming up behind her. She didn't say anything in response like I expected her to. As I waited for her to answer, I stepped onto a bridge of rocks someone made before we had found the stream, making crossing easier.

"Morgan," she started, and then immediately stopped and sighed. I looked at her silently. She had been doing this kind of thing for a couple months now, and I was slowly becoming accustomed to it. "You know that I love you like a sister, right?"

I could only nod, focusing a good portion of my energy on sticking my arms out at my sides so I wouldn't topple into the water.

"But I don't know if we can still be friends."

At that, I almost did fall in the water.

"What?"

Jamie sighed again. "It's just … I don't know. I can't tell you why, even though I really wish I could. My life is really complicated right now." Another deep, heavy sigh that sounded like it came from deep in her soul. "I'm stuck between a rock and a hard place right now, Morg, and I don't want you to be stuck with me. It's a dangerous place."

I hopped from the rocks and onto the dirt again to sit beside her on the log.

"Maybe I want to be stuck with you," I argued.

Jamie shook her head. "No, you don't. Especially since you don't even know what the hard place is."

I shrugged. "Doesn't matter. I'll get stuck with you so we can kick the hard place, whatever it may be, right in the butt."

Jamie smiled. It wasn't a real Jamie smile, but it was better than the sighs, so I let it slide. She gave me a quick, one-armed hug.

"Thanks, kid."

Kid? Jami never said stuff like that. But as with the phony smile, I didn't say anything and just hugged her back.

I mentally cursed myself. I should have seen the signs. The change in her attitude, her speech. I shook my head to get rid of the thoughts and focused on the troubling thought that the memory brought: mine and Charlie's growing friendship was not a good idea. It was too dangerous for Charlie.

Another car drove by. No, it was the same one. It had the same muffled engine sound. It was going the same leisurely speed. I waited for it to drive away. The engine didn't grow faint, didn't fade away. Didn't leave.

I didn't even try to fight the curiosity. I got up and crept over to the window. In the darkness, a familiar white van sat idling right outside our house.

*No*, my mind screamed, *no, no, no, no!*

Chills ran up and down my spine. I closed my eyes against the memories the sight of the van brought, against the old feelings, willing them to go away. They were playing with me, and I knew it.

My shoulder brushed the dark curtain, making it move a fraction of an inch. I opened my eyes in time to see the van's lights grow brighter as it pulled away from the curb and disappeared from view.

# Chapter 17

I didn't go back to sleep that night. I didn't want to dream about Jamie or the people in the white van. So I was downstairs before the sun rose, sitting at the table. Only minutes before, I went through the motions of putting ground coffee in the filter, placing the filter in the coffee maker, and running water through it. Now I was watching the black liquid drip methodically into the pot below—as if there was something even slightly fascinating about it.

"Mmmm, talk about waking up to the smell of coffee."

I swiveled my head and saw Dad standing in the doorway to the kitchen. His sweatpants and T-shirt were rumpled. He had dark smudges under his eyes.

"You only get half," I warned. "The rest is mine."

Dad chuckled and held up his hands in surrender.

"I'll even let you pour my cup so I don't get too much," he allowed. I nodded affirmatively. He pulled up a chair and sat next to me.

"What are you doing up so early?"

I arched an eyebrow. "I could be asking you the same thing."

"Some of us work." He stood up to pour himself a cup of coffee, completely forgetting that he promised me I could do it.

"It's Sunday."

"You caught me." Dad sipped his coffee.

I slouched in my seat, arms crossed over my chest, clearly saying: *Well? I'm waiting.* He leaned against the counter.

"I went in to check on you, and you weren't in your room."

He tried to hide it, but the worry in his voice was unmistakable in a way that strangely reminded me of Charlie.

"I've been down here the whole time." *Nothing's going to hurt me.* But I didn't add that part. My mind jumped back to the white van and reminded me that I couldn't make a promise like that.

"I just wanted to make sure." Dad sounded defensive. He scrubbed a tired hand over his face. He needed to shave. Part of me, the little bit of the person I used to be that still lurked deep inside me, wanted to jump up and hug him. In the end, the new me won, and I couldn't even muster a comforting smile.

The atmosphere in the kitchen turned awkward. I got up and silently got myself a cup of coffee, closing my eyes to savor the hot liquid running down my throat and warming the inside of my belly. When I opened them again, Mom was making her way to join us. Her eyes flickered to me, then Dad, then back to me.

"You two are up early." But that's all she said on the matter. She got some coffee, closing her eyes to savor the flavor just like I had a few minutes ago. No one said a word.

The shrill ring of the telephone shattered the silence. I jumped up to grab it, thankful to whoever it was for providing me a distraction from my parents.

"Hello?"

"Morgan! You're really awake?"

I rolled my eyes when I recognized the voice. "No smart-alec, I'm asleep. What do you want?"

"Ha! My theory was a success!"

"What theory? Really, Charlie, I'm not in the mood."

"The theory that Morgan Casey is grumpy in the morning." I could almost hear the grin in Charlie's voice. I had the most ridiculous urge to laugh, but I held it back.

"Okay, so you proved your theory. Can I get off the phone now?" I silently prayed he would say no; I didn't want to hold a conversation with either of my parents.

"No."

I breathed a sigh of thanks.

"Believe it or not, I didn't call just to make fun of you and your morning moodiness."

"I don't believe it," I teased. Then echoed, "'Morning moodiness?"

"Now who's the smart-alec? And yes, morning moodiness."

"Well then, what do you want?"

"Well, I thought it'd be nice to inform you of our busy day ahead."

"Our busy day?" I asked, incredulous that Charlie planned my whole day out for me. I didn't know whether to be irritated or grateful.

"Don't interrupt," Charlie halfheartedly chastised. "Now listen, I'm on my way to your house—"

"You're what?"

Charlie sighed. "What did I tell you about interrupting? Anyway, once I get to your house, we're going to pick up your car. Then we're going to take it back to your place and drop it off. After that, I'm going to show you there's more to Mistle than school and the little kid's barber shop."

I was intrigued. "And you didn't feel the need to run any of this by me because …?" I left the question to hang in the air.

"I knew you would say no. I'm starting to figure you out, Morgan Casey." There was a click then a dial tone.

I hung up and walked to the window in the living room, pushing the curtain aside so I could see outside. Sure enough, Charlie's electric blue sedan was parked confidently in the driveway. Charlie was beaming at me from behind the wheel. Smiling, I rolled my eyes and let the curtain fall back into place before bolting upstairs to get in something that wasn't pajamas.

A few minutes later, I was calling over my shoulder, "Mom, Dad, I'm going to be gone all day! I'll call if I need anything!" before going out the door.

I found Charlie leaning against the hood of his car, his lips pulled back into his signature smile, showing off a perfect row of pearly white teeth like his mom's.

"I'm tired of you waking me up in the morning." I tried to sound convincing, but I was sure my smile was betraying me.

"Get over it," Charlie said gently. I laughed and got in the driver's seat. Charlie came to the door and tapped on the window. I rolled it down.

"What?"

"What do you think you're doing?"

"Getting ready to leave without you if you don't get in," I threatened. Charlie chuckled and shoved away from the door. A few seconds later, he was sitting beside me and giving me directions to the auto shop. That's when I realized I'd been smiling for more than a few seconds.

I was slowly starting to see colors again.

# Chapter 18

"Well, miss." The portly mechanic wiped his grease-covered hands on a rag that I'm sure was once white in color and straightened up to look at me. He nodded toward my Pontiac. "That thing yours?"

I nodded and wished that Charlie was there so he could do the talking for me.

I remembered the surge of panic I felt when Charlie had excused himself to the bathroom just after we arrived at the auto shop. That meant I was going to have to be alone with a stranger. Even if it was only for a few minutes, it still frightened me.

The mechanic shook his head sadly and stared at my car. "You sure get a lot of use out of it, don't you?"

My hands were shaking, and I balled them into fists, stuffing them in my pockets. "What makes you say that?" I wondered if the fear in my voice was as evident to him as it was to me.

"Your spark plugs were completely missing, like they'd fallen out or something."

Could spark plugs just fall out of a car? I didn't think so.

"And your brake wires were almost completely cut. You're lucky you couldn't get the car started, because if you had, you wouldn't have been able to get it stopped."

I took my hands out of my pockets to wrap my arms around myself. Whoever had sabotaged my car had done it to make sure I didn't get home that night.

"I guess I got lucky then," I mumbled.

The mechanic nodded emphatically. "That you did." He paused for a second. "Say, you got any enemies?" Then he chuckled to himself like it was a joke. And it was—to him.

I felt a strong hand in the small of my back, and Charlie stood beside me. I breathed in a sigh of relief, feeling like a huge weight had been lifted off me.

"This girl? Have enemies?" Charlie snorted and grinned. "Not likely."

The mechanic smiled mischievously at us, which immediately made me bristle and step away from Charlie's touch.

"How much does she owe you?" Charlie asked, watching me curiously out of the corner of his eye.

The mechanic bit the side of his lower lip to think. "Does one hundred twenty-five dollars sound fair?"

Charlie looked at me, and I nodded slightly.

"Sounds very fair," he said.

"I can just send the bill to your house so your folks can pay for it," the mechanic offered. "I'm just going to need your address. Then you won't have to worry about it."

A little voice in the back of my head told me it was a bad idea to be giving my address to anyone, even if he was just the friendly neighborhood mechanic. But when Charlie nodded encouragingly at me, it seemed like there was no such thing as a bad idea.

I took the form that the mechanic handed to me and filled out my name, address, and phone number (just in case he had to contact us about anything, he told me). Then he handed me my car keys and disappeared in the back of the shop.

Charlie nodded at me. "I'll follow you back to your place in my car. Then we can hit the mall or something—and I'm driving."

I started toward my car. "What makes you think I want to go to the mall?" I asked over my shoulder.

I didn't have to see Charlie shrug to know he did it. "Because you're a girl. Don't all girls like the mall?"

"Some of them." I climbed in my car and rolled down the window to keep talking to him.

"How about you?"

"Sometimes. Are there any good movies out?"

Charlie's laugh echoed through the garage. "You can be very demanding. First ice cream and now a movie."

"I didn't ask for ice cream."

"No, you didn't," he admitted.

I started the car and slowly started driving out of the garage. Charlie moved out of my way and gave me a little wave.

"We'll go check out the mall, and then we can go bowling or something. My treat. Hey, I'll race you to your house!" Charlie called after me. He sprinted for his car and had it started in no time.

That was all the incentive I needed. I beeped the horn to let him know that I was up for the race, and then gunned the gas and tore out of the parking lot, ready to see exactly what my little car could do.

I risked a glance in the rearview mirror to see Charlie right on my tail and about to pass me.

Suddenly, I jerked the steering wheel to pull over. I watched Charlie do the same and come to an abrupt stop right behind me. He got out of his car and leaned in my window just like a police officer would.

"What's wrong?" he asked.

"We're going to get pulled over for drag racing," I warned him.

"Or speeding," Charlie added in a completely serious voice, even though he was smiling.

I playfully smacked his arm. "Thanks for the help. Anyway, I'm already dreading telling my parents that they're going to get a bill for the repair of my car that they didn't even know was broken—"

"Your parents didn't know there was something wrong with your car?"

"And you yelled at me for interrupting," I teased him. "But no, they didn't know about it and they still don't and I don't want to have to go home with a ticket too."

Charlie sighed. "I get what you're saying. Okay, no more racing." He tapped my door with his knuckles and got back in his car.

I let him pull out first, and when he was going nice and slow, waiting for me to follow, I pressed the gas pedal to the floor and sped ahead of him. Behind me, I heard him honk his horn, long and loud, before following in hot pursuit, and we raced back to my house.

# Chapter 19

In the end, I beat Charlie to my house. By the time he pulled in the driveway, I was sitting on the front lawn, absently plucking blades of grass. I didn't look up at him until his shadow loomed over me.

"What took you so long?"

"Some cheater tricked me, and then I got stuck in traffic. It wasn't my fault."

I grinned at him. "This cheater, do I know them?"

Charlie shook his head in mock seriousness. "No, you don't. She's very clever, devious almost, and guarded ..."

I kicked him.

"And abusive," he added with a laugh. He offered his hand to help me up. I ignored it and got to my feet myself.

"So what now?" I asked, crossing my arms over my chest.

"You give the FBI a call."

"I did this morning," I lied.

Charlie regarded me with a thoughtful expression before finally saying, "No, you didn't. Let's go." He started for the front door, and I jogged to catch up with him.

"I hate you," I muttered halfheartedly.

Charlie laughed at me. "Why?"

*For seeing right through my lie.* "For making me call the FBI."

"It's just a precaution. Aren't you into those kinds of things?"

I didn't answer and just pushed the door open. As I let Charlie into the kitchen, I heard raised voices from the living room and prayed that Charlie wouldn't ask questions. He didn't.

Wordlessly, I reached into the freezer and pulled out an ice tray, very conscious of Charlie's gaze the whole time, and smashed it against the counter until the ice exploded into a hundred little pieces. In the bottom of the tray sat a little Ziploc baggie. I opened it and withdrew a slip of paper. I spun around to see Charlie staring at me with one eyebrow raised. I held the slip of paper up between my index and middle finger.

"FBI agent's cell phone number," I explained.

"Why was it hidden in an ice tray?"

"Safety precaution." I pointed to the wall across the room. "The phone's over there. Will you get it for me?"

Charlie walked over and grabbed the wireless phone off the wall and brought it to me. "Way to prove my point."

I disregarded his comment and started dialing. One ring. Two rings. Three.

"Grant," A voice on the other line grunted.

"Hello, Agent Grant. It's Morgan Casey."

I heard him sigh heavily, and that made me grin.

"Hi, Morgan. Why are you calling me?" His voice changed, like he covered up the mouthpiece. "Hudson! Get your gun out! Do you want to be killed?"

"You sound like you have your hands full," I commented.

"We're working on a very delicate hostage situation right now, Morgan, with very serious killers; I can't afford to be talking on my cell. What do you want?" His voice was steady. I could tell he was trying to keep his patience.

I shot Charlie a mischievous grin. "Oh, nothing. I was just calling to see how you were doing."

"Morgan!" Agent Grant growled.

"I thought they didn't let you in the FBI if you had a bad temper. I guess there's a first for everything." I pressed my lips together to keep from laughing. Charlie was doing his best to shoot me a disapproving look, but I could tell he wanted to laugh just as much as I did.

"Morgan Casey, I will hang up this phone right now and never answer it again if you don't tell me why you called. I swear it!" He must have covered up the mouthpiece again. "I'm tired of this! Just kick down the stupid door!"

"It's not nice to swear," I told him.

"Oh my God, someone call an ambulance!"

I heard Agent Grant yelling a few choice words.

"Wow—you really do have your hands full."

"Yes, I really do." His voice sounded funny, like his teeth were clenched. "So you're going to tell me why I'm talking to you instead of helping my partner deal with a major crisis right now."

He was done playing this game with me, and I knew it, so I cut right to the chase. "Have you guys caught the creeps who kidnapped me last year?"

"No, we haven't." His voice softened. "I'm sorry, Morgan, but we think they're back in Russia. And if they are, there's nothing we can do. Why?"

"Because my friend and I were being followed by an SUV with tinted windows yesterday, and there was a white van sitting outside my house around two this morning, and I want to know why." I glanced at Charlie. He had this look on his face that was close to panic, but not exactly there yet. I'd forgotten to tell him that part.

There was a pause. Then Agent Grant swore loudly. "That means they might not be where we can't get them. Morgan, I need you to be careful. They could be after you. Once I'm done dealing with this, my partner and I will take care of everything. Bye." There was a click, and I knew he hung up.

Angry, I pressed the end button. That was it? No, *thanks for keeping us informed? Don't worry, they won't get you?* Nothing? Just a, *be careful, we'll take care of everything?* Right, just like they "took care of everything" by letting those jerks get away last year. I slammed the phone on the counter then ripped up the slip of paper and threw the pieces away.

Silently, Charlie reached into the trash can, pulled out the shredded pieces of paper, and tucked them in his sneaker.

"What'd you do that for?" I grumbled.

"It's still pretty much legible, and we need that connection."

I rolled my eyes. "They're no help at all. No, we don't."

"What did he say?" Charlie asked.

I shrugged. "I have to be careful, and once they get done with whatever they're doing now, they'll take care of everything." I snorted. "Please."

"They'll do their best," Charlie assured me. He stepped toward me, arm outstretched, and I moved around him.

"What if their best isn't good enough, Charlie! They couldn't stop me from being taken last time, and they're not going to be able to stop it this time either!" I half-walked, half-ran, toward the living room.

"What are you doing?" Charlie called after me.

So many words were running through my head. I had to make sure I said the right ones out loud. "I'm going to tell my parents we have to move again. It's not safe anymore." I didn't really see what was going on. All I saw was flashbacks of last year, and then the SUV following me and Charlie, the white van outside my window. I wasn't thinking clearly.

"Whoa, whoa, whoa." Charlie's arm snaked around my waist and pulled me back into the kitchen. He had me pinned against his chest. I pounded my fists into his arm, and he grabbed them with his other hand. I tried to bite into his wrist and kicked at his legs.

"Let me go," I hissed, still straining to hurt him. To force him to release me.

"Morgan, calm down," he said into my ear. Didn't yell, didn't whisper. Just, kind of … told me. Like he was talking to his little sister in that soothing voice of his. "Please," he added.

The tone of his voice, the way he was talking to me, immediately had a calming effect on me. I stopped fighting him, defeat making me sag against him and letting him support all my weight.

"Good girl. Just calm down. It's going to be all right." He was whispering now, but he never loosened his hold on me. My breath hitched. My chest heaved. I gasped for air. All of me was shaking. "I'm going to let you go now. Promise you won't do that again?" I nodded. Slowly, Charlie let me go. Releasing my hands first, and then removing his arm from my waist. I stood up straight so I wasn't leaning on him anymore.

He didn't ask me if I was okay, and for that I was eternally grateful.

I was breathing normally now. The shaking had disappeared. The flashbacks stopped.

I turned around to face Charlie. He was looking at me with something like sympathy, which I hated. Finally, with his lips pressed into a firm line, he grabbed my wrist, and I followed him outside, allowing him to lead me back into a world of pretending.

# Chapter 20

Even when we got to the car, Charlie never let go of my wrist. He still didn't trust me, but I hadn't given him a reason to, so it didn't bother me. I watched him open the passenger door and let him gently push me into the leather seat. And, although I was perfectly capable of doing it by myself, I let him buckle my seatbelt too. By the time he was in his seat and had the car started, I hadn't moved an inch. My hands were fists in my lap. I was still filled with this anxious energy.

"Calm down." Charlie reached over and grabbed one of my fists, placing it on the middle console and smoothing it out.

"I am calm."

Charlie took his hand away and put it back on the steering wheel. While keeping his eyes on the road, he said, "I find it funny that you still think you can get away with lying to me." He was smirking.

I rolled my eyes and looked out the window for a long time. "You haven't even known me that long." It was a little too late for a comeback, especially one as lame as that, but it was better than letting him think he won.

"A week?" Charlie asked.

I thought back to the first day of school and shook my head. "Not even that. More like a few days." Had it really only been a few days?

"Huh," Charlie said, acknowledging the fact that I could be right. "Feels longer."

It felt kind of loaded to agree with him, so I didn't say anything. I think Charlie sensed my discomfort because he said, "Where to?"

"Surprise me." I didn't really care where we went, as long as it got my mind off of my conversation with the FBI agent.

"Yes, ma'am." Charlie looked at me out of the corner of his eye and caught my smile. He had a glimmer of satisfaction in his eyes when he looked back at the road, like he was mentally congratulating himself on a job well done. I couldn't decide if that annoyed me or made me want to smile bigger. In the end, I dismissed both and stared at my hand still resting on the console, while my other was still a tight fist in my lap.

Charlie started tapping a beat out on the steering wheel. I rested my head on the window as he started whistling along with his beat. The paved road beneath us disappeared, and a dirt road replaced it. I looked at the clock on the radio and wondered what time we left my house so I could figure out how long we'd been driving.

"Where are we going?"

He stopped whistling long enough to answer me. "You told me to surprise you." Then he was back to whistling.

I wasn't going to even bother trying to get it out of him because I knew he wouldn't tell me no matter how much I begged.

Eventually, Charlie pulled off onto the side of a road and got out of the car. But I stayed seated, looking around in wonder. Everywhere I looked: trees, trees, trees. Trees on both sides of the road, and up a little further was a mountain, lush and green because of the leaves. Charlie tapped on my window and gave me an impatient look. Reluctantly, I got out of the car to join him.

"What were you doing?" He was already walking toward the green wall of plants.

"Looking." I took one more peek around before racing to catch up to him.

Charlie chuckled and ducked under a branch. I ducked after him. "At what?"

"Everything. I've never seen anything like it."

"They're just trees. You can't tell me they don't have trees in California." We were tromping through dead leaves and sticks now. Charlie was ahead of me, breaking branches once in a while to clear a path.

"They have trees," I said defensively. "But where I lived, there weren't many, and there was nothing like this."

I watched the back of Charlie's shoulders go up then down. "If you say so."

"I do say so."

"All right then."

We walked without saying anything. Everything was so alien to me, and I had to be careful that I didn't get so caught up in the scenery that I lost Charlie.

"Getting tired yet?" He called over his shoulder.

"No."

He laughed because he knew he caught me lying—again.

"Don't worry, we're almost there."

"Almost whe ..." My voice trailed off when Charlie sidestepped so I could see what was in front of us. My breath caught in my throat.

We were standing on the edge of a thick circle of trees. And to the other side of that circle was a small waterfall on the face of a cliff, falling into a good-sized stream and flowing away. Disappearing into the forest. When I tore my eyes away from the water, I saw an old picnic bench, and beside that was a rusty swing with one of the chains broken, so one side of it lay on the dark, damp ground. The whole area was shaded. It looked like a setting from a movie. Or a book. It didn't belong in this world. It was too beautiful. Too magical-looking.

Charlie walked toward me and grabbed my wrist, careful to avoid touching my hand, and pulled me to the middle of the circle. "What do you think?"

"It's gorgeous," I breathed, for lack of better, more descriptive words.

"My mom used to bring me here when I was younger." There was a sort of sadness to his voice. "I like to come here to think. Because of the serenity."

Serenity. That was a good word to describe the magical place Charlie had brought me to. He didn't say anymore, just let me marvel at what surrounded us. Then he dropped my wrist, and after walking to the stream, he fell to his knees, cupped his hands, and drank the water. I joined him.

"Is that safe?"

Charlie shrugged. "Dunno. I've been doing it for years and haven't gotten sick yet, so I guess so." He stood up to kick his shoes off then stepped into the water. I follow suit, wincing as the cold water rushed over the tops of my feet and numbed my toes, rocks piercing the soft skin that was the bottom of my feet. Charlie laughed at the look on my face.

"You get used to it."

I didn't feel the need to say anything.

This was a place where things could be left unsaid.

I think Charlie thought the same thing, because he didn't say anything either. Until he pointed to the swing.

"I remember the day I broke it."

I blinked at him.

"It was only a few years ago. I was alone. Mom had to stay home with Jenny because we couldn't afford a babysitter anymore. I was swinging as high as I could when it just snapped. I hit my head on a rock and had to walk all the way home with a bloody head." He brushed his fingers on the left side of his hairline. "I only needed four or five stitches, but it still hurt like crazy."

I just looked at him, envious because he could freely talk about his past and I could not. Finally I asked, "Did it hurt?"

He gave me a funny look. "Yeah, a lot. I just told you that."

I shook my head. "No, I mean when your dad left."

"Oh," he said softly. "Kind of. He wasn't around much, but I was still young, and he was still my dad."

"Why did he leave?" I knew that I was probably making him relive painful memories, making him talk about things he'd never really talked about, but I wanted to know why he was who he was. What made him, him.

"I don't know. I think about that a lot. I just woke up one day and Mom was crying and he was gone. All his stuff was gone. A lot of money was gone. He didn't even leave a note." Charlie sat down in the dirt and trailed his fingers through the water thoughtfully.

I sat beside him, watching his face intently.

"Maybe he was just tired of us, or he wanted his money to himself, because he took about half our money out of the bank. No one ever found him. I don't even know if he's still alive."

Charlie didn't sound too broken up, and I was glad because if he did, I'd feel incredibly guilty.

"When I ran away that one time, I looked for him for a while, and when the police brought me back home, I decided I didn't care if I ever saw him again. It's funny because we're doing better without him than we did with him. I'm glad I don't have to listen to him and Mom fight anymore."

I wondered if I was going to be in Charlie's position in a few years. If, eventually, one of my parents would get sick of fighting and worrying over me and just up and disappear without a word. I wondered if I'd be able to be like Charlie and be glad they left.

Charlie took my silence as an end to the conversation and tugged on my arm, standing up.

I looked up at him. "What?"

"I'll be right back. Don't slip and hit your head."

I shot him a withering look before he disappeared back into the woods. I reached my hand into the water and pulled out a flat stone. Then with a flick of my wrist, I sent it skipping across the water before it finally sank. I repeated this process until Charlie returned, rusty metal bucket in hand. He sat beside me several inches away and set it between us. Curious, I peeked in the bucket, and then after seeing the contents, hungrily reached my hand in and popped one in my mouth.

"You don't even know what it is, and you're eating it," Charlie said, seeming a bit taken aback.

I narrowed my eyes. "I know what it is." I held one up for him. "It's a raspberry." Then I popped that one in my mouth too and grinned at him before getting another handful of the red little berries. Charlie watched me eat with raised eyebrows.

"You like raspberries, don't you?"

"I like a lot of things," I said in between chewing the raspberries. "But I like these the most."

Charlie laughed a little and got a handful of his own to eat. "Well, don't eat them all. I want some too," he warned playfully.

"Whatever," I said and dug in the bucket for more.

# Chapter 21

Leaving the circle in the woods was harder than it probably should have been. It wasn't physically hard. Charlie and I just followed the trail we made when coming in. It was just that if I had my way, I'd stay there, dipping my feet in cold water and eating raspberries forever. But Charlie insisted on taking me home—some nonsense about my parents worrying about me. Which wasn't really nonsense when I remembered their reason for worrying about me, but it still made me feel better to say it was. I was jerked out of my thoughts when Charlie abruptly stopped, causing me to run into his back.

"Charlie! What are you—"

"Shhh!" Charlie clamped his hand over my mouth and pulled me to the ground.

"What?" We were both lying on our bellies, the earth under us soft and damp.

"Shut up!" he whispered harshly.

I shut up.

Silently, Charlie pointed out toward his car. I had to squint to see in the growing darkness, but when I did see, I felt sick.

Two people, both clad in dark clothing that covered everything except their hands, ski masks over their heads and faces, and a blade in each of their hands. They were whispering, so I couldn't hear what exactly their voices sounded like or what they were saying. With a nod to each other, they kneeled down, brought the blades to the back tires, and slashed them. They repeated this process with the two front tires then got on two motorcycles and drove out of sight.

I tasted bile in the back of my throat. My stomach was queasy, and I was dizzy. The scene replayed over and over in my head. I was shaking again, and I curled my fingers around dirt in a pathetic attempt to control it. I felt thankful to the shrubs and trees for providing coverage. Thankful to Charlie for noticing them and making me shut my stupid mouth. If I had been alone, I would've walked right into them. I couldn't bear thinking about that. I took a deep breath and turned my head to look at Charlie. He looked a little pale, either because of the darkness or fear. I couldn't tell which. I couldn't find my voice to talk to him, and even if I could have, I had no idea what I would say. It took a long time for him to look at me, and when he did, he forced a smile.

"Some kids take pranks way too far." He stood up and started walking toward his car. I scrambled to my feet and followed him. Being out in the open, surveying the damage to Charlie's car made my stomach churn. The cool night air suddenly felt several degrees colder than it had ten minutes ago. I wanted to turn on my heel and hightail it back to Charlie's circle. They wouldn't find us there. We'd be safe. I'd be able to live without fear of them and eat my raspberries until I threw up. But I knew Charlie would never go for that.

"They didn't look like kids to me," I said.

"Well, they were," Charlie said forcefully, making me wonder who he was trying to convince—me or himself. "Big kids," he added.

Neither of us said anything more because he wasn't that much better of a liar than I was. Instead, he kneeled by a tire and inspected the slash in it, shaking his head.

"How are we going to get home?" I asked.

Charlie pulled a cell phone out of his pocket and checked it. I knew before he told me. No service.

"We walk." He pocketed his cell phone and started toward civilization. I didn't have any choice but to walk with him. The distant roar of motorcycle engines rooted us in our place. It grew louder, and Charlie went to grab my wrist, missed, and grabbed my hand instead. I didn't have enough time to respond before he said, "We run," and started dragging me after him as he sprinted down the road. The fear made it hard for me to move my feet, but Charlie never let go and never slowed pace.

The engines kept getting louder, and when we saw headlights, Charlie dove into the woods, leading us in deep enough so anyone on the road couldn't see us, but we could still see them.

I tried to move as quietly as Charlie did without slowing down but just couldn't. Running almost silently through the woods was an acquired talent, I learned. We were both panting hard, and I was loudly snapping twigs under my feet every time I moved. The headlights grew brighter, the engine louder, until the motorcycles on the road were parallel to us in the woods. It had to have only been for a second or two, seeing how they were on automobiles and we were on foot, but it felt like hours, and I could've sworn one helmet-clad head looked directly at us before they sped past.

They were going the way we came from. Probably planning on sitting and waiting for us. They'd be surprised when we never showed up.

Finally, Charlie slowed down, and we were walking again. I had a cramp in my side. Charlie was panting like a dog and, like me, desperately trying to get air in his lungs.

"That—was—way too close," I panted. Charlie just nodded. We spent the rest of the long walk home trying to catch our breath. Never stopping, never going back to the road. And never dropping hands.

# Chapter 22

We were almost to my house. Halfway down the block, I could faintly hear raised voices coming from my house. Even with a sidelong glance at Charlie, I still couldn't tell if he could hear them or not. He didn't act like it, so I hoped that meant he couldn't hear them. When we reached my porch, he let go of my hand and lightly touched my arm.

"Listen to me. Don't worry about my car, okay? It was probably nothing."

I stared up at him. "How long are you going to keep telling me that all this stuff that's been going on is 'probably nothing'?" I felt tears well up in my eyes, a delayed reaction from today's stress, and forced them back.

Charlie sighed, put his hands in his back pockets, and said, "Until we both believe it."

"It's just too many coincidences, Charlie." I was shaking my head. "With everything that's happened in the past couple days ... look, this is getting dangerous. Just back out now while you can." *Like I should have a year ago.* I almost added that part. I should have, I really should have, and I wasn't sure why I didn't.

He gave me a short laugh. "Are you kidding me? I just finally got you to open up to me, and you think I'm gonna bail?" It was his turn to shake his head. "There's no way you're getting rid of me that easy."

I wanted to argue with him about me opening up to him. But the more I thought about it, the more I realized that he was right. He knew almost as much about me as I did. Wow, so much for my "Staying Safe by Being a Loner" plan.

Suddenly, the sound of a door slamming came from inside. I winced as Charlie looked at the house with concerned eyes.

"I better get inside," I said, surprised that my voice sounded … reluctant.

Charlie stood up straight as a pin and said in a very serious, un-Charlie-like voice, "Be careful, soldier." Then he saluted me. I laughed—part of the reason being that, because it was so out of character for Charlie, it was very funny. The other reason being that I needed that, something to make my parents' constant fighting seem like a lighter situation than what it really was.

I saluted him too. "Will do, Sergeant."

Charlie grinned, did a little wave, jumped off the porch, and jogged out of sight. Smiling, I shook my head at his antics before turning toward the door. With a deep breath, I pushed it open, having no idea what exactly I was walking into, but ready for it either way.

# Chapter 23

It completely amazed me how Mom and Dad didn't even try to hide it anymore. I made my presence known when I came in, slamming the door behind me and stomping into the hallway where they were standing screaming at each other. This one was different. Worse than usual. Something about me being so late—but I didn't see why they'd be yelling at each other for that. They just ignored me for a good twenty seconds. I felt my face getting hot, my temper flaring until I just couldn't take it.

"Oh. My. God. Shut up!" I screamed. Their shouting stopped. They abruptly turned to look at me.

"Morgan Nicole Casey—" My mom started to chastise me for my disrespectful words, but I wasn't done.

"You two just don't know when to stop, do you? You're both acting like little kids!" I was very literally seeing red in my fury. "Don't you get sick of fighting? Ever? My God, one would think you actually like to fight!"

"Morgan!" Dad looked really disappointed in me. Strangely, I didn't feel an ounce of regret.

"Shut up! I have to listen to you two all the time, but you can't listen to me for once?"

"Not when you're yelling like this," Mom said calmly.

I rolled my eyes. "Please. Don't even talk to me about yelling. You argue for a stupid reason. Me! You argue over me!"

Everything about the way Mom was interacting with me softened. "Oh, baby, you're not a stupid reason."

"I am when it's been going on for a year! I'm home now! I'm safe and sound and trying to forget everything, but because of you two, my 'loving' parents, I just can't do it." I held out my hands for them. "Do you see why I want to forget? Why can't you try to forget too? Do you realize that they burn every time I have to think about it?"

"We know what you've been through. We know what you're going through now." Dad sucked at being sincere.

I stared at him with a look of utter disbelief and thought, *There is no way he just said that.* It should have made me angrier, but eerily, it calmed me. I had a ridiculous urge to laugh at him. Laugh at both of them for being so stupid. I narrowed my eyes at him and shook my head, pitying him. My tone was so frigid; my mouth almost felt like it was full of ice. "You will never know what I've been through or what I'm going through right now, at this very second. You didn't have to see your best friend murdered in cold blood right in front of you then wake up every day knowing the monsters that did it are still out there. You didn't have to be interrogated and tortured for eleven days. You don't have to be afraid of people you don't know, and you don't have to worry about endangering your new best friend—who just happens to be the best person in your life right now. No, you have no idea what I have to live with every ... single ... day."

I wanted the conversation to end there. I was so far past done I didn't know what to do with myself. I should've felt bad for the looks of guilt painted across my parents' faces, but I didn't. I felt triumphant for making them feel like scum. I felt lightheaded and giddy for finally letting it all off my chest. I felt like a terrible person.

I needed to get out of there.

Quickly, I spun on my heel and dashed out the door. I only took a second to decide which way to go. Cool air hit my face, and my sneakered feet thudded heavily on the sidewalk as I ran. Any other night, I would've taken the time to admire what was around me. The night sky was full of stars. A black blanket full of little tiny holes. The moon was full, and even at a quick glance, I could see the almost invisible craters in it. It offered enough light for me to see so that I wasn't falling all over myself, and I reminded myself to mention to Charlie how much I loved full moons.

Charlie's house was right up ahead. I could only see one light on in what I supposed was the living room. A shadow pulled back the curtain to look outside. That shadow had curly hair. I was a few yards away. Charlie stepped onto the porch and waved. Even from far away, I could see the question written on his face. In his eyes.

Car headlights came from behind me. My parents coming to get me. To talk to me. Even though I didn't want to, I stopped running and turned around. My breathing sped up, and I wanted to bolt, but fear held me in place.

I should have known better.

A white van. The one from outside my window. The one from my nightmares. The one from last year. It stopped, a door opened, a scream welled up in my throat—but before it could leave my lips, something hit my forehead.

Hard.

The last thing I heard was Charlie yelling. The last thing I saw was a sneering face in front of me.

I was unconscious before I hit the ground.

# Chapter 24

*Oh my God, my head is killing me.* Waking up, that was my first thought. Painfully, I sat up and looked around. My next one was: *this is not good.* First of all, it smelled. Bad. Like a million different barn animals had lived in this dark place, and no one had cleaned up after them. Next, the heat was suffocating. *What am I doing here?*

Someone moaned. And it wasn't me. At least, I didn't think so. As my eyes grew more accustomed to the darkness, I could faintly make out a lump a few feet away from me. An animal maybe? I propelled myself back, farther away from the strange lump. The cement floor felt cold on my skin, and the grains of dirt stuck to the palms of my hands.

Huddled in a corner, I found that I couldn't remember anything.

A light flickered on. I blinked rapidly at the sudden brightness then just closed my eyes altogether. The lights made my head hurt more.

"Open your eyes, girl."

God, I knew that voice. I didn't want to open them. I didn't want to see who I knew was standing in the doorway. My hands felt like they were on fire.

"Are you deaf now?" the voice snarled. "I said open them!"

Hesitantly, I opened my eyes, squinting because of my growing headache.

A woman, tall and slender and dressed all in black, expensive-looking leather stared at me from the doorway. Though she was looking at me with something like revulsion, her lips curled into a very cruel, very evil smile.

"Do you know me?"

Of course I knew her. I didn't know her name, but I knew her. How could I forget?

"Well, do you?" She was frowning now. I was taking too long to answer.

"Well, duh," I said, my sarcasm hiding the fear that was making my whole body tremble.

She smiled again, waved her finger at me, and tsked, "That smart mouth of yours got you into trouble last time we saw each other, did it not?"

I wasn't going to answer that one.

"You are very disrespectful, child. Perhaps your friend will take your punishment for you?"

Friend? Then it hit me, and I felt so stupid. My eyes darted to the lump on the floor. Charlie, just a heap of curly hair, pale skin, and baggy clothes lying on the cold floor. But still Charlie.

"No, he won't." I couldn't tear my eyes from him. I should've looked her in the eye so she would take me seriously, but I couldn't.

"Yes, he will," said the heap. Charlie started to sit up, moaned, and then threw up. I scrambled to my feet and dropped again beside him.

"Children are so putrid."

I looked at her to see her looking at Charlie with disgust in her eyes and her nose scrunched up.

"As if it didn't smell bad enough in here without his vomit." She turned to go and waved her hand dismissively. "One of the boys will come by to clean it up." Then she was gone. The door slammed shut, and the lock clicked in place. At least she left the light on for us. Charlie's eyes were closed, and he was lying on his back.

"Is she gone?" His voice sounded weird. He was trying to talk without opening his mouth too wide.

"Yeah, she's gone. You shouldn't have sat up like that. They must have chloroformed you. Nausea: one of the aftereffects."

"What about headaches?" he mumbled.

"That's one too."

"Who was she?"

I contemplated telling him. If I did, he would know what kind of trouble we were in. I didn't want to face that reality yet. "You need to sleep the side effects off. I'll tell you when you wake up."

He forced his eyes open. I cringed because it looked hard to do. "No, you'll tell me now. I want to know whose fault it is that I just puked and have a killer headache." He was trying to sound funny, but he was angry. Very angry.

I rocked back on my heels and grabbed the toes of my feet. "She's one of the ones who took me last year. The leader, actually."

Charlie digested this. "Hm. She looks so breakable."

"She's not. Trust me, she's not. You should feel special, Charlie. I didn't get to meet her until she killed my best friend." The sarcasm tasted bad in my mouth. Being there made me sick to my stomach.

"Yeah, I feel so loved." Charlie rolled his eyes. I smiled a little. But just as quickly as it appeared, it was gone again.

"I'm sorry I got you involved." Guilt ran through my entire body from the top of my head to the tips of my toes. Mixed in with that was fear. And somewhere in the midst of all that was anger. "You shouldn't be here."

"I wanted involved, remember?"

I almost smiled because he was trying to cheer me up even though it wasn't working.

"It's my fault," he said. "I'm just too nosy, right?"

I shook my head, disagreeing with him. "I'm sorry," I said again.

Charlie touched my arm. "Don't be. It's not your fault they took us."

I opened my mouth to talk.

"Don't argue," Charlie said before I had a chance. I closed it again. "Good girl. Now, how are we going to get out of here?"

"You aren't."

It was a male voice that drew my attention to the doorway this time. He was a big dude. His dark shirt looked too small for him, like his muscles would tear it or something, and his hair was buzzed. His Russian accent wasn't completely gone, like his leader's, but you couldn't detect it unless you were looking for it. The thing is, I was looking for it.

"I did last time," I taunted. I knew this one too.

"We won't make that mistake again," he warned. In his hand, he had a roll of paper towels and a metal trash can. "Who vomited? I've been ordered to clean it up."

"That'd be me, no thanks to you." Charlie slowly, hesitantly sat up and looked him defiantly in the eyes.

"Stupid American boy, you should have known not to move before the effects wore off."

"You should have known not to chloroform a beginner kidnap victim," Charlie shot back.

The man threw the metal trash can at him. Charlie ducked, and it landed harmlessly a few feet behind him.

"Watch that mouth of yours," he warned before picking up the garbage can. Without saying anymore, he cleaned up Charlie's mess and left.

"Real friendly folks here," Charlie noted. "Wherever here is."

"You haven't even met the third one. He's one you'd want to have at a party." Joking around like this was making me feel a bit better. I was still scared, but I was starting to think clearly again. "We have to be in a barn somewhere."

Charlie's face said: concern. "The closest barn I know of is hours from Mistle, Morgan. This isn't looking any better." Charlie looked down at his feet, and for the first time, I did too—only to find them bare except for my thin socks. "Why'd they take our shoes?"

I swallowed hard. "Keeps us from running," I said quietly. "Can't run fast without shoes, can you?"

Whatever light mood Charlie had been trying to create a minute ago was completely gone. He stared hard at his sock feet. "Are we ever going to get out of here?" He said it so softly that I came close to missing it.

I almost wished I had, because I didn't have the answer I knew he wanted.

# Chapter 25

"You look different," she said. I glared at the woman who held me and Charlie captive.

"As do you," I said, tone cold, teeth gritted. I was annoyed at her for toying with us.

She smiled, pleased with herself. "What'd you do? Dye your hair? Is that really all?"

I nodded.

She sighed and shook her head. "You should have done more, girl. It would have kept us away longer." She was gloating. They found me, and they had me, and they won. "But it wouldn't have kept us away forever, so don't beat yourself up about it too bad. No point in holding off the inevitable, am I right?"

"No," Charlie interjected.

She leveled her stone gaze on him even as she spoke to me. "Your friend's mouth is almost as bad as yours was. We may have to take care of that."

He gave a short laugh like he didn't believe she was serious. He opened his mouth to add something, but I set my hand lightly on his arm, and he stopped.

She smiled cruelly at me. "You've learned, haven't you? You know better than to antagonize us."

I didn't say anything. Didn't move.

She gave a little disappointed sound. "Well, since you refuse to make small talk with me, we might as well get down to business." As she said it, two men appeared silently behind her. One of them was the one who threw the garbage can at Charlie. The other was one I knew too well. He had dark hair under a hat I didn't see the point in. He wore a loose coat to hide the menacing muscles I knew were there. His face was blank, expressionless. "You do know why you're here, don't you?"

"I'm assuming this isn't just a friendly reunion," I said, accompanied by an eye roll. The big one stepped forward, only to be held back by the woman's scrawny arm.

"We won't use him unless you give us another hard time," she warned.

"Gee, thanks," I said sarcastically.

The three of them inched closer to me and Charlie.

"Are you ready to tell us what secrets your friend sold?"

"Charlie didn't sell any secrets." I had to say it, to mess with them longer. It was too tempting not to. The big one stepped forward again, and this time she didn't hold him back. He slapped me across the cheek, hard. Tears sprung to my eyes, but I held them back. *God, that's going to be an ugly bruise later.*

Charlie sprang to his feet, fists clenched at his sides.

"Sit. Down," she said before he could do anything. "Or he will hurt her again." Charlie sat down.

"It didn't hurt," I mumbled. With the look Charlie shot me, it was obvious he knew it had hurt—and hurt bad.

Big Guy—that was a good name for him (even though it lacked creativity)—cracked his knuckles. "I'll make it hurt."

I shrugged it off, and a fire blazed in his eyes. At his boss's word, he would snap my neck. I needed to watch what I said.

"Now," she said, "maybe I wasn't clear enough. Tell us what secrets your late friend sold."

The way she said "late" caused my eyes to narrow and my hands to form fists. "Maybe if you'd ask nicely."

Her smirk was bone-chilling. "I don't need to ask nicely, girl. I have someone ready to kill you with a snap of my fingers if you don't tell us."

I shook my head. "You won't kill me. You need me, remember? If I were to die, you'd never know the secrets."

She paused, thinking about my point. "Very true." Something sparked in her eyes, and I wished I'd just kept my mouth shut.

"How important is your friend to you, Morgan? Would you break an old friend's promise to save a new one?"

Before I could answer, Big Guy had grabbed a handful of Charlie's curly blond locks and hauled him to his feet.

"You wouldn't." They would. She gave a nod, and Big Guy slammed his fist into Charlie's belly. First I heard the sound of flesh hitting flesh, and then Charlie's moan. I wanted to turn away, but Charlie's eyes found and held mine. They screamed: *pain!*

"Stop." My voice sounded weak. It was a plea, but I didn't care.

Another punch. Then another.

"Stop!" I yelled.

It stopped. Charlie had his head bent now, breathing hard, wheezing.

"We're perfectly serious, Morgan Casey."

I couldn't look at her.

"Are you hearing what I am saying, girl? We will kill him, just like we killed your other friend. We will get what we want; I can guarantee that."

Big Guy dropped Charlie, a dull thud against the concrete. I winced. A door slammed, and when I looked up, they were gone. I crawled over to Charlie. He was on his side, his legs pulled up to his chest, arms wrapped around himself. Sweat dampened the edge of his hair.

"Charlie, oh God, I'm sorry." I rested my forehead on his cheek and closed my eyes. "I'm sorry."

"Don't be," he choked. Somewhere in the back of my throat, a painful lump formed, and I tried hard to swallow it. "You're doing the right thing."

"Look at you," I whispered. "This can't be the right thing."

"Didn't you know that doing the right thing hurts?" he asked, and then cringed. "Really bad."

"Let me see." I sat up so Charlie could lay flat on his back. Carefully, I lifted his shirt. His belly was already decorated in dark bruises. There wasn't any skin left that wasn't colored black and purple.

"Is it bad?" he gasped.

I put his shirt back down. "Not as bad as it could be." *But still bad.*

"Okay."

"They're not done," I warned him. "They'll be back."

It was a few heartbeats before he spoke again. "I know."

# Chapter 26

"What time is it?" whispered Charlie.

I shrugged. "Your guess is as good as mine."

"Sometime in the morning maybe? We've been here the whole night at least."

That sounded about right. "Sure."

"Are they going to feed us?"

My stomach growled at his question. "Once every two days probably. That's what it was last time."

"So, tomorrow then?"

"Yeah, maybe." I took a moment to take in our surroundings. We were definitely in a barn of some sort. To my right were two horse stalls, and on my left were bales of hay piled on more bales of hay. The metal door was around the corner of the horse stalls. They must have had this place in mind long enough to replace the door. It wasn't a spur-of-the-moment kidnapping; that was for sure.

"We need to figure out a way to get out of here," Charlie said.

I nodded. "Let's see, one door, no windows, and nowhere to hide but the horse stalls. It doesn't look good."

He heaved a sigh. "I know. It was just a thought."

"And a good one too."

I looked toward the door where the woman and the two guys were standing. They could come in here too silently for my liking.

"But unfortunately not possible," she added, coming closer.

"That's what you think," I said, sounding much more confident than I felt.

"That's what I know," she snarled. "You aren't getting out of here. Get over it."

I scowled at her. Out of the corner of my eye, I saw Charlie edge away from her and felt guilt pound me like angry waves. Big Guy grabbed Charlie's hair again so he was standing.

"What secrets did your friend sell last year?" the woman asked.

I felt defeated. If it were me getting beaten for my insolence, I wouldn't care. But Charlie didn't deserve that. I exhaled slowly. "Jamie—"

"Don't tell them, Morgan!" Charlie yelled. Big Guy backhanded him on the cheek, but he pressed forward. "I can take it, okay? I won't be mad at you. Those secrets are yours now. Keep them bottled up." That awarded him a punch, full in the mouth. I looked away when I saw blood well up on his lips. "They're yours," he said again through the blood.

"He's so noble," she mocked. "Now, if he's done with his rude interruption, you can continue your story."

I kept hearing Charlie's words over and over in my head. *Those secrets are yours now.* I looked her right in the eye and shook my head. "No."

Immediately, my eyes flitted to Charlie. Big Guy twisted his arm and pushed it up behind his back. Charlie gasped in pain and bit his already bleeding lip to keep from crying out. After a few long seconds, Charlie got his arm back. "Good girl," he whispered to me. I swallowed and nodded.

"I'm getting tired of this game," the leader said. "Next time we come back, I want secrets."

Big Guy dropped Charlie and then kicked him just for the cruelty of it, before the three of them disappeared into whatever was outside that door.

"How's the arm?" I asked sympathetically.

Charlie scooted beside me and cradled it. "Sore, but it's okay. I'm proud of you for keeping your secrets. I know it must have been hard."

"I don't like seeing them hurt you," I admitted.

"Then don't watch. But we're gonna get out of here eventually, secrets and all. Until then, I can take a few bumps and bruises." When I didn't say anything, he changed the subject. "Have you noticed that the one that came in here to clean up after me last night doesn't say anything? He just hangs back behind the other two and stares at the floor?"

This news startled me. "Really?"

"I don't think he wants to be here anymore than we do."

"You know what? I think you're right. So why do they bring him in to begin with?" I asked.

Charlie shrugged. "So they outnumber us? That would make sense."

I took a second to process this. "We could use that to our advantage. Do you think he's armed?"

"Most likely. Yes, I think so. So if things get out of control, he can help the other two, who like to use their hands instead of guns."

"Sounds logical." That conversation ended there, both of us lost thinking about this new revelation.

"Do you think someone's looking for us?" Charlie suddenly asked.

"Yeah," I answered immediately. "I know for a fact that my paranoid parents must have called someone by now."

"I wonder how Jenny's doing." If the news that someone must be trying to find us was making him feel better, he didn't act like it.

"I'm sure she's fine. Probably misses her big brother like crazy, but fine."

Charlie gave the air a sad smile. His mind was somewhere else. I took his hand, and the invisible fire on my hands was extinguished instantly. He never looked at me, just squeezed my hand and returned to his thoughts.

# Chapter 27

"Morgan!" Charlie's excited whisper woke me from my restless slumber.

I sat up instantly, ready to face whatever was happening. Hurriedly, I looked around. And finding nothing too out of the ordinary, I whispered back,

"What?"

Charlie was shaking in his excitement. He wore a grin I hadn't seen since the first couple days of meeting him. A grin that didn't belong there, in the situation we were in.

"I didn't change my socks!"

I waited a beat. "Um, ew?"

Charlie shook his head and waved his hands. "No, no, no. Do you remember when you called the FBI agent?"

I nodded, not following.

"And you got mad and ripped up his phone number? Then I picked it out of the garbage and stuck it in my shoe?"

"Yeah, so? They took our shoes."

"It slipped into my sock!" Charlie paused for dramatic effect. "And you wanna know something exciting?" He didn't wait for me to answer, just leaned forward to whisper clandestinely. "I still have my cell phone!" He leaned back and smirked.

I stared at him, realizing the importance, but not being able to fully wrap my head around it. This happened in movies. Other people got lucky like this, not me.

"Are you serious?" was all I could manage. He nodded, looking like a little boy. Suddenly, I laughed. "They are so stupid!"

"Shh!" Charlie whispered, half-laughing. "I know. But we're gonna be grateful for it!" Quickly, he pulled his phone out of his pocket, took the shreds of paper out of his sock, and got to work putting them together on the floor. He looked up once to say, "It's a good thing you suck at shredding stuff."

Any other time, I would have hit him. But in my giddiness, I laughed.

"Let me do it." I took his phone and started dialing the digits. To say I wasn't scared that we'd get caught would be a huge lie. I was terrified, but the adrenaline masked a good amount of that fear, and I hoped that even if we did get caught, rescue would come before something bad happened.

"Who's this?" I'd never been happier to hear Agent Grant's deep, cool voice.

"Morgan Casey," I whispered.

"Oh my God, Morgan! Where are you?" I heard him call to someone who must have been in the room with him. "It's the Casey girl! Turn it on!" He was back to me. "Morgan, don't move, okay? Are you all right? Can you tell me where you are?"

"We're both fine—" He cut me off.

"We?"

"Charlie is here too. My friend. We're okay considering. You have to come. We're in a barn somewhere ..."

The door flew open, and my stomach dropped to my feet. All three of them were standing in front of me. She looked angry, ready to kill. Big Guy looked like he wanted to laugh. The other one looked like he wanted to cry.

"Morgan, are you okay?" Agent Grant's voice was very much in control, but I could detect a bit of worry. "What's happening?"

She leaned in close, so her face was inches from mine. Her breath was cold and minty. "Hang. Up. Now," she said through gritted teeth.

"G-grant. I-I have to go," I stuttered.

He swore. "No, Morgan. No, stay on for just a little longer. What's going on?"

Violently, she yanked the phone from my hand, snapped it closed, and chucked it against the wall where it shattered.

I risked looking at Charlie, his face white as white, staring shell-shocked at the three evil people in front of us.

She slapped my cheek. "Who was that?"

I smiled a little, even though my cheek felt on fire. "An FBI agent. You guys are toast."

She gave a loud cry of rage and gave Big Guy a significant look. He grinned and cracked his knuckles before grabbing Charlie and viciously pulling him up.

"Right now, Morgan." She was looking at me again. "You'll tell me right now!"

"No, I won't."

That earned Charlie a punch. I heard his nose crack. As if in slow motion, blood seeped out. Dripped down his lips, his chin, before falling and splattering on the concrete. Forever staining it a rusty red and giving it the horrid memory of the violence that occurred here.

"You'll risk his life to keep a few secrets? You're some friend!" she yelled.

"Why do you want to know anyway?" I yelled back. "They already know the secrets! You can't do anything about that, so just let us go!"

"Do you not know anything?" Her English was slipping a bit in her fury; I could hear a faint accent. "We want to destroy those people so they can tell no one else!"

The thought made my stomach churn. I wasn't going to give them reason to kill more people, even though they were part of the reason Jamie was dead. I just couldn't do it. "You are never going to know enough to take their lives," I said defiantly.

"I've lost my patience!" she shrilled. "Arthur, kill the boy!"

For the first time, I felt extreme panic. Names. They were using names. They were really going to kill Charlie, and then me when they were done with him. A cruel smile slowly spread on Arthur's face, and he kneed Charlie, who groaned and doubled over.

Using Charlie's golden hair, Arthur straightened him back up, just to push him down again. Without warning, he picked Charlie's head up and slammed it on the concrete. Hearing the loud crack, I screamed. Blood flowed fast from the side of his head. Somehow, his eyes found mine. He should have looked angry at me, or in pain, or sad. But he kind of smiled at me until Arthur landed him another punch in the stomach. I forced my eyes from his and looked at the leader, seeing that she was distracted by Arthur and Charlie. Then I stared at the third one. He looked sick.

"Come on, Art," he begged. "You don't have to kill him."

In a split second, I knew what I had to do. Everyone's attention was focused solely on Arthur beating Charlie. Silently, imperceptibly, I crawled so I was behind the third one. Just as we thought, he had a small handgun tucked in the waistband of his jeans. Without giving it a second thought, I pulled it out and trained it on Arthur with a steady hand. Just as he was about to bash Charlie's head against the concrete again, I pulled the trigger.

# Chapter 27

Arthur landed on his side with a thud. Both the leader and the third guy had whirled around to look at me, their jaws slack. I aimed at her, then at the third one, then back to her. I couldn't find my voice.

"FBI! Don't move!"

The door banged down, and a dozen or so armed women and men wearing bulletproof vests ran in the room. They grabbed the remaining two and tugged them out of the room before I knew what was happening. My whole body relaxed in relief. The gun clattered to the floor.

A couple of medics were bent beside Charlie, who was barely hanging on to consciousness, while a few others carried Arthur out of there.

I slid to the ground and rested my forehead on my knees.

I couldn't have been sitting there long before a woman with a red, straight ponytail bent down next to me. She gently touched my arm.

"Morgan, I'm Agent Smith." She smiled at me. "How are you doing?"

I didn't answer. Staring off into space, I said, "Is Arthur dead?"

She nodded sympathetically. "Yes, he is. I heard you shot him. Got him straight in the back of the head. He died instantly."

"Am I in trouble?"

"No, I also heard it was to save your friend. You made a hard decision, but it was the right one, Ms. Casey. Your friend is very much alive."

I looked at her, disbelieving. "But there was so much blood," I whispered.

She smiled and ruffled my hair. "Head wounds tend to bleed pretty bad even if there isn't much damage. Our medics wrapped his head and his ribs, put some medicine on his split lip. He could have a concussion and broken ribs, definitely a broken nose, but he wants to see you before he goes to the hospital." She cupped my elbow in her hand and pulled me up to walk me outside.

The driveway was full of black vehicles and ambulances. The white van was there. Charlie was sitting on the grass beside the barn, looking up to talk to the distinguished man I knew as Agent Grant. I sat down beside him, and they both looked at me.

"Are you okay?" Charlie asked me.

"Are *you* okay?"

He grinned. "Never been better."

I smiled and shook my head at him. "Right." I looked at Grant. "How'd you find us?"

"We had a tracker on your call. You weren't on long enough for us to know the exact location, but you mentioned a barn, and this is the only barn in the area."

"Thank God for their stupidity," I breathed.

Grant nodded. "You can say that again. We want to take you both to the hospital, but there's no hurry, so take your time."

"My parents?" I asked.

"And my mom and Jenny?" Charlie added.

"All of them are waiting at the hospital. Let us know when you're ready. You two did well." Then Grant walked away. When he was gone, Charlie looked at me and took my hand.

"Thank you for not telling them your secrets," he said. Then he whispered in a voice that was just for me, "And thank you for saving me."

I stared at him. "Charlie, I killed a man." Then, for the first time in a year, I burst into uncontrollable tears.

"Morgan," he said, and pulled me into his lap even though I felt him wince as he did so. "You had to, Morgan, you had to."

I cried into his shoulder, getting his shirt that smelled like bad memories wet. *He was evil,* I told myself. *He deserved to die. He killed Jamie. He was going to kill Charlie.* I didn't think it was possible to feel so guilty but so relieved at the same time. "I wish he didn't make me kill him," I sobbed.

Charlie kissed my ear reassuringly as he whispered, "But he did. You can cry, because that's what's right. But in the end, you didn't have a choice." As my sobs died down, he lightly kissed the top of my head. I hid my face in his chest. "Is it time to start getting back to normal?" he asked.

Sniffling, I wiped my eyes. "Let's go see our families," I answered.

He pulled me up with him and took my hand. And this time, instead of leading me back into a world of pretending, like he did earlier, he was leading me into a world that was finally safe again.